VE FEB 2011
EN JuN '13
SU Feb 17

The Baron of Coyote River

OS JAN 2018
KD OCT 2018

SELECTED FICTION WORKS BY
L. RON HUBBARD

FANTASY
The Case of the Friendly Corpse

Death's Deputy

Fear

The Ghoul

The Indigestible Triton

Slaves of Sleep & The Masters of Sleep

Typewriter in the Sky

The Ultimate Adventure

SCIENCE FICTION
Battlefield Earth

The Conquest of Space

The End Is Not Yet

Final Blackout

The Kilkenny Cats

The Kingslayer

The Mission Earth Dekalogy*

Ole Doc Methuselah

To the Stars

ADVENTURE
The Hell Job series

WESTERN
Buckskin Brigades

Empty Saddles

Guns of Mark Jardine

Hot Lead Payoff

A full list of L. Ron Hubbard's
novellas and short stories is provided at the back.

*Dekalogy—a group of ten volumes

L. RON HUBBARD

The Baron of Coyote River

GALAXY
PRESS

Published by
Galaxy Press, LLC
7051 Hollywood Boulevard, Suite 200
Hollywood, CA 90028

Printed in the United States of America.

ISBN-10 1-59212-304-X
ISBN-13 978-1-59212-304-9

Library of Congress Control Number: 2007928018

Contents

Stories from Pulp Fiction's Golden Age

AND it *was* a golden age. The 1930s and 1940s were a vibrant, seminal time for a gigantic audience of eager readers, probably the largest per capita audience of readers in American history. The magazine racks were chock-full of publications with ragged trims, garish cover art, cheap brown pulp paper, low cover prices—and the most excitement you could hold in your hands.

"Pulp" magazines, named for their rough-cut, pulpwood paper, were a vehicle for more amazing tales than Scheherazade could have told in a million and one nights. Set apart from higher-class "slick" magazines, printed on fancy glossy paper with quality artwork and superior production values, the pulps were for the "rest of us," adventure story after adventure story for people who liked to *read*. Pulp fiction authors were no-holds-barred entertainers—real storytellers. They were more interested in a thrilling plot twist, a horrific villain or a white-knuckle adventure than they were in lavish prose or convoluted metaphors.

The sheer volume of tales released during this wondrous golden age remains unmatched in any other period of literary history—hundreds of thousands of published stories in over nine hundred different magazines. Some titles lasted only an issue or two; many magazines succumbed to paper shortages during World War II, while others endured for decades yet. Pulp fiction remains as a treasure trove of stories you can read, stories you can love, stories you can remember. The stories were driven by plot and character, with grand heroes, terrible villains, beautiful damsels (often in distress), diabolical plots, amazing places, breathless romances. The readers wanted to be taken beyond the mundane, to live adventures far removed from their ordinary lives—and the pulps rarely failed to deliver.

In that regard, pulp fiction stands in the tradition of all memorable literature. For as history has shown, good stories are much more than fancy prose. William Shakespeare, Charles Dickens, Jules Verne, Alexandre Dumas—many of the greatest literary figures wrote their fiction for the readers, not simply literary colleagues and academic admirers. And writers for pulp magazines were no exception. These publications reached an audience that dwarfed the circulations of today's short story magazines. Issues of the pulps were scooped up and read by over thirty million avid readers each month.

Because pulp fiction writers were often paid no more than a cent a word, they had to become prolific or starve. They also had to write aggressively. As Richard Kyle, publisher and editor of *Argosy*, the first and most long-lived of the pulps, so pointedly explained: "The pulp magazine writers, the best of them, worked for markets that did not write for critics or attempt to satisfy timid advertisers. Not having to answer to anyone other than their readers, they wrote about human beings on the edges of the unknown, in those new lands the future would explore. They wrote for what we would become, not for what we had already been."

Some of the more lasting names that graced the pulps include H. P. Lovecraft, Edgar Rice Burroughs, Robert E. Howard, Max Brand, Louis L'Amour, Elmore Leonard, Dashiell Hammett, Raymond Chandler, Erle Stanley Gardner, John D. MacDonald, Ray Bradbury, Isaac Asimov, Robert Heinlein—and, of course, L. Ron Hubbard.

In a word, he was among the most prolific and popular writers of the era. He was also the most enduring—hence this series—and certainly among the most legendary. It all began only months after he first tried his hand at fiction, with L. Ron Hubbard tales appearing in *Thrilling Adventures, Argosy, Five-Novels Monthly, Detective Fiction Weekly, Top-Notch, Texas Ranger, War Birds, Western Stories,* even *Romantic Range.* He could write on any subject, in any genre, from jungle explorers to deep-sea divers, from G-men and gangsters, cowboys and flying aces to mountain climbers, hard-boiled detectives and spies. But he really began to shine when he turned his talent to science fiction and fantasy of which he authored nearly fifty novels or novelettes to forever change the shape of those genres.

Following in the tradition of such famed authors as Herman Melville, Mark Twain, Jack London and Ernest Hemingway, Ron Hubbard actually lived adventures that his own characters would have admired—as an ethnologist among primitive tribes, as prospector and engineer in hostile climes, as a captain of vessels on four oceans. He even wrote a series of articles for *Argosy,* called "Hell Job," in which he lived and told of the most dangerous professions a man could put his hand to.

Finally, and just for good measure, he was also an accomplished photographer, artist, filmmaker, musician and educator. But he was first and foremost a *writer,* and that's the L. Ron Hubbard we come to know through the pages of this volume.

This library of Stories from the Golden Age presents the best of L. Ron Hubbard's fiction from the heyday of storytelling, the Golden Age of the pulp magazines. In these eighty volumes, readers are treated to a full banquet of 153 stories, a kaleidoscope of tales representing every imaginable genre: science fiction, fantasy, western, mystery, thriller, horror, even romance—action of all kinds and in all places.

Because the pulps themselves were printed on such inexpensive paper with high acid content, issues were not meant to endure. As the years go by, the original issues of every pulp from *Argosy* through *Zeppelin Stories* continue crumbling into brittle, brown dust. This library preserves the L. Ron Hubbard tales from that era, presented with a distinctive look that brings back the nostalgic flavor of those times.

L. Ron Hubbard's Stories from the Golden Age has something for every taste, every reader. These tales will return you to a time when fiction was good clean entertainment and the most fun a kid could have on a rainy afternoon or the best thing an adult could enjoy after a long day at work.

Pick up a volume, and remember what reading is supposed to be all about. Remember curling up with a *great story.*

—Kevin J. Anderson

KEVIN J. ANDERSON *is the author of more than ninety critically acclaimed works of speculative fiction, including The Saga of Seven Suns, the continuation of the Dune Chronicles with Brian Herbert, and his* New York Times *bestselling novelization of L. Ron Hubbard's* Ai! Pedrito!

The Baron of Coyote River

CHAPTER ONE

False Bullets

THE man who came from across Hell's Parade Ground was stumbling, weaving from side to side in the wagon tracks, dragging up a yellow curtain of lazy dust behind him.

His high-heeled boots were battered, his angoras were heavy with mud long since dry, his yellow hair was matted from an old wound.

But he still walked and he still had his saddle. The saddle alone told its story. Here was a rider without a mount, here was a puncher who had come far.

And those who watched him come from the shadowy 'dobe of Santos read his story long before he had arrived.

If this man came from nearby he would wear leather batwings, and he would have had better sense than to stab at Hell's Parade Ground afoot in August. And the men of Santos reasoned with narrow eyes that this man was an outlaw—and as such they would receive him.

Lance Gordon did not care what they thought of him. He was too spent and hot for that. The sizzling sun made him feel like a roast pig, lacking only an apple to be served at a buzzard's banquet.

He stumbled through the outskirts of the 'dobe settlement, swerved into the main stem and limped toward a place facetiously named the Diamond Palace Saloon. The twenty-nine-inch tapaderos trailed from the saddle behind him but the silver conchas were too smeared to shine.

He stopped for a moment in the sun and looked into the dim bar, then, taking a hitch in his already frazzled nerve, he made the last ten feet, to lean wearily against the mahogany.

The half-breed bartender left off polishing glasses. "Name your poison, stranger."

Lance Gordon paid no heed to the stray punchers who had gathered curiously at the door. With a heavy effort, he plumped the saddle down on the bar, giving it a push.

"How much will you give me for the rig?"

"I ain't buyin' rigs, stranger."

"It's Mex and it's worth plenty. Look here, I'll let you have it cheap enough."

"Sorry, stranger. But," he added with a calculating muddy eye on the saddle, "I might let you take it out in trade."

"You got a gun . . . and maybe some ammunition?"

"Well, a feller kicked off here last week and he kind of bequeathed me his gun as sort of payment on his bar bill."

"Make it the gun, plenty of bullets and a quart and it's a trade."

The bartender pulled the saddle toward him, noticing two bullet holes in the skirt. In its place he planted a belted Frontiersman Colt .45. He grudgingly added the bottle.

Lance Gordon heard a wondering murmur from the doorway and he glanced sideways without any great interest at the silhouettes of the punchers against the bright yellow sunlight outside. He picked up the gun and buckled it about him, pocketed the cartridges and took the whiskey bottle by the neck. Then, stumbling against tables, he made his way to the far corner of the room and sat down with his back firmly against the wall. That was another bad sign.

A tall man with a heavy black beard and colorless eyes came in and leaned up against the bar. He wore batwings of extreme design which bore down their length gaudy spades, hearts, clubs and diamonds. At the sides, lashed down tight and low, were two pearl-handled, gold-chased revolvers of late pattern. The hat was straight brimmed and stiff and he wore it rakishly. For all the expression and movement he made he might as well have been a rock butte jutting out of the desert.

"Come far, stranger?" said this one.

Lance Gordon frowned heavily and raised a drink to his lips, his hands shaking until the amber fluid slopped over his knuckles.

"You never can tell," said Lance.

Another murmur came from the doorway. Two men importantly shouldered their way through and took their stand in the center of the room. One was wearing a black vest and a dirty white shirt, the other wore a star glittering against a coat the color of dust.

"I'm sheriff here," said the man with the star. "Brant's the name."

"Not *the* Brant," said Lance with an unsteady smile.

Brant shoved his chest out a little. "That's me."

"Never heard of you," said Lance.

The tall bearded one smiled.

Brant scowled until his little pinched eyes were almost invisible. His gray mustache bristled. "I came in here to find out what your business was in this town, stranger."

"That's easy," said Lance. "My business."

Brant took a step nearer, peering intently at the newcomer. He saw a disk of silver sparkle on Lance's chin thong and on closer inspection knew that the sparkle came from a set diamond there.

Brant began to smile and inch his fingers toward his gun. "I know you now. Your name's Lance Gordon, ain't it? I'd know that thong anyplace. You might as well come along peaceable-like. Don't seem they appreciated MacLeod's killing over in the Sierras."

Outside of an almost imperceptible tightening of his muscles, Lance received the news calmly. "Word travels fast, doesn't it?"

"About killers," said Brant, fingers closing over his revolver butt.

It did not seem to those who watched that Lance Gordon moved, but the gun he had just received from the bartender looked like a tunnel about to receive a train.

"I'm tired of running," said Lance. "I'm sick of it. It doesn't matter to you that MacLeod slaughtered a dozen men to get his land in the Nevadas. If you've got orders to send me back, then carry them out. But I'm not going—alive."

Brant stepped hastily back. The bearded one against the bar smiled again.

"There's plenty to take you over at the fort," promised Brant.

"Then send for them," said Lance, bitterly. "I've walked fifteen miles since my horse died. I'm tired. It shouldn't take more than a company to get me."

Still backing, Brant made the door, but there he was suddenly heaved inward again by pressure from without.

Into the room came a blue-coated, brass-buttoned cavalry officer followed by troopers who held ready carbines in their hands. The group came without a word, walking stiff-legged as though to a firing squad. Their black, wide-brimmed hats were salted with gray dust and their boots were almost white.

"Howdy, Captain Anderson," said Brant. "I'm glad you came over. That's Lance Gordon over there."

Anderson turned a thin, harsh face toward his man. "I heard about it. I've had telegraphic orders for two days. Forgot about the new telegraph, didn't you, Gordon?"

Lance poured himself another drink and tipped his chair back against the wall. "Well, what are you waiting for? Sure, I shot MacLeod and I knew you'd have orders. But if I still had my horse, you'd have to look all over Mexico to find me. But I didn't have my horse very long and now I'm doing you a favor. Come on, why don't you take me?"

He spun the revolver by its trigger guard, idly.

Captain Anderson turned to his troopers. "Take him, men."

The revolver leveled itself. "I think," said Lance casually, "that I might as well have a military guard to hell. Come on, gentlemen. Do you want to live forever?"

The troopers hung back. Anderson grunted and unbuckled his own holster flap.

Lance stood up, throwing the chair to the floor. He steadied himself against the table and glared at them. "Come on," he begged.

The carbines dropped to port. The troopers nervously glanced at their captain and then stepped closer to Lance.

Gordon pulled the trigger, but instead of the blasting roar of a Colt came a small snapping sound. He stared dully down at the weapon, failing to understand. The troopers pressed ahead, knocked the revolver away and quickly grasped Lance by the arms, dragging him forward.

The bartender snickered, "Think I wanted to lose my best customers? Them's duds he's got there."

Lance was sagging but he glared all the same.

Brant began to laugh with nervous relief. "Now we'll see about it. Now we'll see. What are your orders, Captain?"

"I'm to hold him here for trial and then execute him." He buckled his holster flap again and said, "Come on, men."

The tall bearded man at the bar cleared his throat. "I beg your pardon, fellers, but I wouldn't go no place if I was you."

The group halted, astounded, and stared into the muzzles of those flashy twin guns.

"For God's sake, Tyler, have you gone crazy? Put those things away. This ain't your fight." But Brant stayed where he was nevertheless.

Captain Anderson barked, "March."

"Halt," said Tyler. "Let loose of that feller."

Anderson grew red with anger. "This isn't your quarrel, Tyler, and I'm tired of your pranks. Get out of the way."

"Nix," said Tyler, grinning through his black beard. "This

is the first guy I've seen with guts in three months. You ain't takin' him anyplace whatever. Son," said Tyler to Lance, "you'll find a cayuse outside all saddled. You go out there and get going and don't let no jackrabbits pass you goin' north. I'll see you up near Coyote River this time tomorrow."

Lance shook himself free. He was smiling. "Thanks, pardner."

Anderson tried to hold Lance, but Tyler solemnly cocked his Colts one after the other. Lance went outside.

"I'll get you for this, Tyler," yelped Anderson.

"The hell you will," replied Tyler. "You'll be plenty nice to me or Washington might hear something about the dough you owe around here. Get going there, Gordon. That bronc with the rimfire saddle."

Lance mounted, sunk his spurs, applied the quirt and went out of Santos to the roar of kettle-drumming hoofs.

CHAPTER TWO

The Baron

A LL through the next morning, Lance Gordon lay under a clump of brush beside the dry streambed known as Coyote River. A canteen and a sack of food had been tied to Tyler's saddle and he had breakfasted well upon jerked beef and pemmican and two swallows of water. And then with a good night's rest, he felt like he had lost twenty years of age.

As do all men who live with the sky as a roof and the earth as a bed, he recovered quickly. He even looked forward to his meeting with Tyler. It was not at all strange to him that Tyler had let him go. Men did those things for no more reason than a whim.

He saw two riders coming lazily up the rocky trail. They smoked as they rode and their hats were low against the beat of the hot dry sun.

For a nervous ten minutes he thought they were on his trail, but they passed by his hiding place without any of the cautious movements which would mark a searching party.

"The Baron'll be sore as hell," said one.

"Yeah, Shorty, we better hit it up or we'll be late. He ain't shot anybody for a week and he shore feels ornery."

They went out of earshot after that, leaving Lance somewhat mystified. He had not been aware of a cattle outfit this far up into the hills and the last time he had come through this country there had been no royalty about that he had seen.

But as the day wore on he lost interest in the Baron and began to be anxious about Tyler. Had the man gotten away after that bold stand?

In the evening twilight he saw a cloud of dust rolling up out of the south, a cloud which marked the coming of more than one man. Again he was apprehensive. He looked dubiously at his Colt, the gun which had failed him. He did not trust it even with a fresh load.

And then he was treated to a very odd sight. Tyler was coming upon a big, long-legged bay, and Tyler was coming fast. Behind him, faint in his dust, the dying sun picked up dots of light—brass buttons.

Tyler raced his mount across the dry streambed of the Coyote River and deliberately stopped. The cavalry came up to the other bank and pulled in. Anderson sat his horse imperiously, one gauntleted hand upon his saber hilt.

"Adios," called Tyler. "Hope you gents enjoyed your ride."

"We'll get you," bawled Anderson. "Stick your face back into Santos and see what happens."

Lance expected to see the troopers dash across the streambed with flaming carbines, but he was disappointed. It seemed as if they had run into a stone wall and could go no further.

Tyler deliberately turned his back upon them and rode slowly up the trail. The cavalry wheeled and went back the way they had come at a slow walk.

"*Hist,*" said Lance.

Tyler looked up and reined in. He cocked a boot around

the low horn of his macheer saddle and deliberately built himself a cigarette. Lance came out of the brush.

"How come they didn't follow you across?" said Lance.

"This is the Baron's territory, pardner."

"What's that got to do with it?"

"Last time they crossed they went back with six empty saddles and they ain't tryin' it again."

"Then are you the Baron?"

Tyler's big laugh boomed through the dusk. He applied a lucifer to his smoke. "No, hell, no. But I guess I'm the one man this side of the border who ain't scared of the Baron."

"Then you're a friend of his."

"Nope, wrong again. Son, don't you go tryin' any of these guessin' games. The Baron would give about five thousand dollars to tack my scalp to his coup stick. But my scalp is still stayin' where she is."

"Then we're on dangerous ground."

"Son, your intelligence amazes me. But here's what I got in mind . . ." He stopped and climbed down. "Let it wait until we poke somethin' into our bellies. You don't think I risked the wrath of the great Captain Anderson just to get a killer out of a scrape, do you?" He glared at Lance, trying to make Lance believe it. "Hell, no, I'm a practical man."

"I guess so," said Lance, grinning.

They dined upon jerky warmed over a smoldering fire and had a couple cups of hot coffee. Then they moved some yards up the streambed and spread their sougans.

Tyler folded his legs under him and built another smoke. "Let's hear your story, Gordon. Then I'll tell you mine. Seems

13

as if we ought to know something about each other if we intend to play our hands right."

Lance shrugged. "It isn't so much of a story at that. I got kind of sore at this MacLeod. He drilled my dad and the shock killed my mother. I drifted out of the country for a few years and then when I heard that this MacLeod was still kicking, I decided some upright citizen ought to do something about it. I went back, walked into him on the street in Los Gatos and give him an even break.

"But I guess Los Gatos kind of reformed since my last visit and the citizens didn't take so well to the killin', brandin' it a murder. I even paid to have MacLeod planted, but that didn't soothe them any.

"And then it turned out that MacLeod was a United States Deputy Marshal, a fact which I carelessly overlooked, and it don't seem to matter none what kind of a skunk a man is, if he wears that badge he ceases to have a price on his pelt.

"So the jail wasn't so strong and I drifted fast, but in going, some pretty good shots got their mark on me and the horse, and the horse didn't last long. I was about done in when I got to Santos. But thanks to . . ."

"Forget it," said Tyler, impatiently. "Didn't I say I didn't do nothin' out of kindness? Me, I ain't got a drop of goodwill in me, don't never think that. Me? I got a use for you, son." He paused for a long while.

Lance stood up. "While- you're thinking up a practical reason, I'll just take a walk up toward the trail and see that nobody is inspecting our fire."

He came back after a bit and sat down again across from the dot of red which pulsated in the blue darkness.

Tyler took a long drag and said, "I dunno whether to let you in on this game or not. I have been havin' such a fine time myself that I hate to share the fun. But it happens that the Baron knows me pretty well and . . .

"This guy they call the Baron is a big chief around here. He drifted in with a stack of bills and a frock coat and a diamond horseshoe pin. Pretty soon he disappears and we don't see him none for quite a spell.

"And then we notices that a lot of gunslingers are drifting through Santos on their way north, and also several gents hereabouts started to complain that their cows were getting plumb lazy and didn't seem to be dropping so many calves as usual. And every once in a while we'd find a Bar T cow bein' tagged by a Three B calf, which is very strange.

"Now this strip of hills up here ain't so big. It don't contain more'n twenty thousand acres, but it's so fixed that it's hard to get to, especially if somebody don't want you to get there. Before now I was running a couple thousand head through here, but one day I didn't have so much as a slick-ear left. Then I find out that the Baron, bein' a softhearted gent, has decided to help me out, thinkin' that I need a rest. And so he takes these cows off my hands and sets his own boys to herdin' them for me.

"That's very thoughtful of the Baron and so I starts in to wipe him up, but instead he plants about five fellers for me. And then Anderson gets word from Washington that this place may be made a state shortly and therefore it's got to be clean. So Anderson rides in on the Baron and, as I said before, comes back with six empty saddles.

"Not that Anderson's to blame. He ain't got but two troops and the government gets plumb absent-minded in sendin' him supplies such as guns and bullets and remounts. There ain't any Injuns to worry about no more and the government thinks this is what it's named—city of the saints. And it might be, if we passed around a few less horns and a few more halos.

"So Anderson don't like this part of the country, and besides, he took a fancy to faro and monte and he keeps busy trying to get out of debt the way he got in. The man ain't to blame, though.

"So when you came along, I was pretty bored, what with the Baron takin' care of my cows for me, and I decided maybe you'n me might team up and do something about it. We ain't got anything to lose, and if we got the Baron's stock and all, when they make this territory a state, then we'd be all set up. They might send us to Congress or something. I always did have a hankering to wear a hard-boiled shirt."

Tyler laid back on his sougan. "That chin strap of yours, son. Seems as if I knew another gent that wore something like it. Diamond set in a silver disk to keep the thong together."

"Sure you have. The gent's name was Windy Green, a terror up around Dodge."

"How'd you get it, pardon my askin'?"

"He and I sat in the same game one night and he thought a full house would beat four kings, and when he got done payin' off the debt—after tryin' to shoot his way clear—he let me have this here chin thong. I always thought it was right pretty until they recognized me by it in Santos."

"Hell, that was part of the description they wired ahead about you via Texas. I thought you was this Windy Green when I seen that thing. He had a rep as a gunslinger, didn't he?"

"Sure, and he wasn't bad either." Lance grinned and touched the thong clasp. "He said he'd meet up with me someday and take this off me again, after which there'd be a planting party."

"Think you could pass yourself off as Windy Green?" said Tyler, suddenly.

"Why, I reckon so."

"Uh-huh. Well, listen, son. Nobody knows the layout of the Baron's ranch well enough to tackle it. Now if you were to go in there, get a job along with the half a hundred riders he's got and map things out, then maybe you'n me could do something to improve the civic pride hereabouts. Besides, I'm plumb lonesome without my cows."

"Suits me," said Lance.

"Never can tell what'll happen. You might get plugged and Windy Green himself might be there."

"I'll take the chance," said Lance.

"Then let's roll in and get some sleep and tomorrow morning you can head up north a ways and get yourself a job."

"Suits me," said Lance casually.

They slid into their hard beds and for long hours Lance lay staring up at the stars listening to coyotes yap along the bluffs. Once a lobo wolf let the world know he was there with a moaning, quavering howl. After that Lance drifted off into slumber.

CHAPTER THREE

The Three B Ranch

BEFORE the sands of the hills became hot, and before the sun had begun its scorching climb up to its zenith, and while the trails were still clear, Lance Gordon and Tyler rode at a trot toward the Three B ranch.

They came to a narrow pass and at its entrance Tyler pulled up. "This is as far as I go with you, pardner. Them fellers know me too well and they shore can play hell with a Sharps rifle. It's your hand from now on and don't let nobody deal you one off the bottom."

"Where'll I meet you again?" said Lance.

"There's a pinnacle of rock a couple miles south. There's a spring of good water up there and you can see for miles. You just give me some kind of a signal and I'll see it and come down near here to meet you. Then, when you've got all the inside track, you and me'll have us a picnic. Meantime, here's luck, Windy Green."

Lance raised his hand in salute and wheeled his horse into the narrow pass mouth. He proceeded briskly through the flat blank walls for a good three miles before he found a break.

"Swell place to get trapped," thought Lance.

He left the narrow defile and rode along a winding trail which led down to lower ground. Here the grass was better due to a small stream which meandered through the valley.

19

It was good grazing land and the Baron had several thousand head wandering through the meadows. The cattle bore all manner of brands, some of them carelessly worked into his own.

"Must trail way north to the railroad," thought Lance, seeing all the different brands. "He's sure got a crust."

He finally came in sight of the ranch buildings. The collection of 'dobe structures were spread out in miniature below him. Men were moving about, and in the corral, the wrangler was herding the remuda together while punchers built loops and picked out the day's victim from their string.

To get down there, Lance had to pass between two great boulders. He was halfway through when a drawling voice said, "You ain't goin' no place, are you, stranger?"

A tall, cadaverous gentleman who chewed slowly upon a bulging cud slouched into sight, Henry rifle across the crook of his arm.

Lance saluted him with a careless wave of his hand. "I heard tell a gunslinger could get a job down here. Anything in it?"

The guard roved his watery eyes over Lance. "You don't rhyme, stranger. Watcha doin' with hair pants and a Texas saddle? And you're a long way off your range with them Spanish spurs. Which is it? California or Texas?"

"You never can tell," said Lance. "Maybe you better let me do my talkin' to the Baron."

"Then drop the barker down," ordered the guard.

Lance left his revolver in its holster. "Lead off to the Baron. We'll let him decide whether or not you get a new gun."

20

Sullenly, the guard called for another man and presently a second puncher rolled up the trail, eyeing Lance distrustfully.

"This pilgrim opines he wants to see the Baron," said the guard. "Take him down."

"Uh-huh, get down, stranger."

Lance dismounted and, with the puncher behind him, walked toward the biggest 'dobe.

At the door he was met by another man who looked him over carefully.

"Feller wants to see the Baron, Fallon," said Lance's guard.

"That's dandy," said Fallon, "but why bring him down here to get shot? Why the hell don't you guys tend to your business up the trail?" Fallon, in a black coat, looked like a crow with its wings folded up. His beak of a nose was set too high between his eyes.

"Maybe, when the Baron finds out who I am, he'll thank you kindly," said Lance.

"Uh-uh. You take him back where you got him, Jim, and ventilate him a little bit. We don't like strangers, down here."

The guard tugged at Lance's arm, but footsteps from within the hut stopped him.

A huge, overbearing man shoved Fallon to one side. This was obviously the Baron. He wore a long frock coat cut like a gambler's, and his buckskin pants, foxed with black leather, were tucked into fancy high-heeled boots. The Baron wore a black, stiff-brimmed Stetson and a black-and-white flowing tie. His face was swollen from bad liquor and his eyes were sucked into his head. He had three gold teeth which sparkled through his black beard. His mouth was thin and cynical, deeply lined on either side.

"What's all this chatter about?" demanded the Baron. "What's the matter with you and Harry up the trail, Jim? Can't you attend to a simple job like that? Who's this man?"

Lance fingered the silver-set diamond of his chin thong. "You might have heard of Windy Green someplace, Baron."

"Windy Green? Why, yes." The Baron looked long at Lance probingly. "I hear you're supposed to be a pretty good shot, that right?"

"You never can tell," said Lance.

"Uh-huh. Where'd you get wind that I wanted men?"

Lance plunged. "Feller in Dodge."

"Might have been Flannery," said the Baron aside to Fallon. "Know the man's name?"

"Nope. Met him in a poker game."

The Baron chewed the end of his mustache thoughtfully. "I got some good riders here. Dunno if I need another."

"If you're sending some of the boys with a trail herd for . . ." Fallon got no farther. The Baron silenced him with a saberlike glance. "See here, Windy Green, I thought you were from down Texas way. What are you doing with angoras and Spanish spurs? Trying to pull something down here?"

"I been over in the Sierras," said Lance.

"Uh-huh. Well, we might use another gunslinger. I've got a couple men I'd like to have killed here. One by the name of Tyler and another named Brant. Too nosey. Think you could do it?"

"You never can tell," said Lance.

"Uh-huh. Pay's six a day and a string of cayuses."

"That's all right," said Lance.

"That's the bunkhouse over there."

Lance took the hint and departed, leading his horse.

When the man was out of earshot, Fallon said, "You should have investigated him better. I know he's got that diamond-and-silver thong clasp, but all the same, this territory may get to be a state most anytime and the government would sure want to clean the place up first. He might be a spy."

"Uh-huh, and if he is, then maybe we can use him. But he might be Windy Green. I've heard tell that man was poison. Tell you what you do, Fallon. You spread it around through the outfit that this may not be the man he says he is. That way, they won't let him get away with anything. But if he is Windy Green, I'm glad to have him. We'll have a tough fight on our hands sooner or later and every gun'll count. Meantime, speed up with that trail herd. The buyers'll be getting impatient up north and we might have to skip out with plenty of cash."

"Right," said Fallon, and followed Lance's course toward the bunkhouse.

During the next few days, Lance had every chance to inspect the Three B ranch, but strangely, none of the punchers or gunslingers seemed to pay any heed to his cautious questions and he finally had to be content with what he could guess.

They were a hard crowd, the Three B. Collected from every corner of that wide-flung range, from the Mississippi to the Golden Gate, they represented the worst of their kind.

In another period when men talked first and let the law shoot it out later, these men would have found their way to the captains of crime and would have been content with the gutters.

But something in the bigness of the Southwest, something in the hard, perilous life they led, had given them a brand of courage which, though it might be classed with the proverbial cornered rat's, was nevertheless a type of valor. They were blustering when they knew they were safe, they were bullying until they were called, they were efficient in a hard-fisted, arrogant way, as long as their leaders were just a little bit harder and tougher than they.

For three days Lance Gordon rode with them, cutting out a trail herd from a dozen different brands, working over Triple Hs and Bar Sevens and Flying Ys into crude Three Bs with the use of wet gunnysacking and running irons. The whole cradle of the valley stunk with the smell of burned hair and wood smoke. The Baron was working fast, getting this herd into shape and away before the word that they were coming preceded them. To the north there was law.

As a matter of cold fact, the Baron and his kind were not too far from their victims. The cattlemen of the wide plains had founded their own herds upon rustled stock from the Mexicans. But with fifty straight-shooting men at his back, the Baron's might made right, and the range, unable to recruit enough rifles, unwilling to die for a few cattle, did not dare protest too loudly when even the two troops of cavalry were powerless against the Baron.

Lance stumbled over his first obstacle in the person of a man named Bat Summers, a fellow six feet tall and all muscle, even between the ears. Bat Summers habitually wore an antagonistic expression, which went with the notched and well-worn butt of his gun.

On the third morning, still groggy with sleep, Lance built his loop and whisked it into the remuda, aiming for a bay of his string. But the light was bad and the rope, thanks to the cold of that high altitude, was stiff, and perhaps Lance, used to open country and a sixty-five-foot grass rope, could not quite accustom himself to a lariat forty feet long. The loop fell short and dropped neatly about the head of a rearing black.

Lance, disgusted, began to take in. A clap of thunder at his side said, "That's my hoss!"

"I gotta free my rope, haven't I?" said Lance.

"I said that's my hoss," repeated Bat Summers.

The man was looking for trouble and Lance gave it to him. In a sudden burst of anger, Lance tossed the end of the tight rope, whip fashion, about Bat's ankles. The black, sensing the looseness, plunged away. The curling rope lashed itself tight and brought Bat's feet out from under him. He sat down hard in the dust, swearing.

"You did that on purpose!" roared Bat.

"Sure I did," said Lance, evenly. "Going to do anything about it?"

Bat leaped up and rocked forward on the balls of his feet, palm flat and going down. Murder flickered in his eyes.

Lance stepped back a pace and sprang to one side, drawing swiftly with a queerly loose motion. Bat's gun belched flame. But before Bat could fire again, Lance had fanned twice.

Bat doubled up with a startled grunt, dropping his gun.

Blood began to run between his fingers as he clutched his chest. Eyes staring with disbelief, he crumpled into the dust.

Lance walked away but Fallon was in his path.

"What's the idea?" said Fallon. "We needed that feller. Cantcha keep your head or what?"

"You lookin' for trouble, too?" said Lance.

Fallon backed hastily away, flapping his arms. "No . . . no . . ."

Lance went on, undisturbed.

The incident in itself was small enough, but it had its effect by bringing Lance to the Baron's attention.

The Baron, that evening, sent for the supposed Windy Green.

"Hear you can't keep your gun in," said the Baron, leaning back in a chair and stabbing Lance with his sucked-in eyes.

"He asked for it, I gave him the break."

"Uh-huh, I know. But funny as it seems to you, Windy Green, I need every man I've got. And now you've made me lose two."

"Two?" said Lance, sensing the presence of other men on the porch.

"You and Bat Summers. Two."

"Y'ain't thinking of anything rash are you?" said Lance.

"Uh-huh. But old Dave Sweeny just carted in a load of chuck and he's going out again in the morning. He says you bein' a friend of his, he'll be glad to take you east a ways, seeing that you don't stop off around Santos. Know him, don't you?"

"You never can tell," said Lance. "But what's the idea shipping me out? I'm . . ."

"I don't care anything about that. But this trouble might start other trouble and it's hard enough to keep gunslingers peaceful."

Footsteps came from the porch and an old man with a white beard looked hazily into the room.

"Come in, Sweeny," said the Baron.

"That you, Windy?" said the old man, peering closely at Lance.

Lance froze. He took in the room quickly. Men on the porch, a saddled horse at the side of the house, a lamp burning smokily upon the table and a window behind him.

"Hell, you ain't Windy Green," said Sweeny.

The Baron rocked forward in his chair, hand racing toward his shoulder holster. Men moved fast on the porch, coming in.

Lance swept up the lamp and sent it crashing against the table. A wall of flame sprang between him and the Baron.

A man fired through the doorway. Lance dived through the window and lit in a rolling heap. Colts roared behind him.

He snatched at the reins, breaking them with a jerk, and sprang into the saddle. He jabbed his spurs into the mount's flanks and hanging low over the horn, shot out across the meadow.

Behind him the hut, half lumber and half 'dobe was bursting into great tongues of flame.

"There's your signal, Tyler," panted Lance, riding hard.

CHAPTER FOUR

Santos Again

THE Baron's office might be burning, but that in no way interfered with pursuit. In the dusk a string of riders lashed out of the camp, riding fast to the crack of romals and quirts.

Lance looked back at them and then up at the entrance to the pass. There, he knew, he would find two guards who would know, merely by looking at the uproar, that Lance must be stopped, preferably dead in his tracks.

But there was no other escape from the valley and Lance could hardly turn back. And so he rode straight at the boulders which might momentarily spew death at him.

The Baron's success, so thought the Baron, depended upon stopping the man who might be a spy. Lance knew that swift bullets already had his name scratched on their blue noses.

The boulders grew bigger and bigger ahead of him. Abruptly two men detached themselves from the rock and leveled their rifles. Involuntarily, Lance checked his horse. The threat of the guns was too plain. Perhaps . . . but it was a wild thought. He couldn't ride them down. They'd gladly drop him at the first sign of resistance. Perhaps other men had tried to escape this way.

Hoofs rolled closer behind him and the line of racing men

began to bunch up for the kill. Once Lance had ridden down a wolf out on the wide prairies. The wolf had looked back at him with hate and fear in its yellow eyes and had finally turned to face an enemy he must have known meant death.

Lance knew now how that wolf had felt and, for a fleeting instant, he was sorry he had killed it.

The tall, cadaverous guard sang out, "Pull in and get down!"

Lance pulled in under the muzzle of the Henry rifle, but he did not get down. The two guards moved closer to him, eyeing him with thin distaste.

"Drop him," said the man known as Harry.

Lance tried to get at his own gun, but he knew that he couldn't make it. Harry's finger was already tight on the trigger.

Suddenly flame and thunder rolled out of the boulders and Lance thought for an instant that Harry had fired. But Harry dropped into the darkness, throwing the rifle away as he went down. The other man, Jim, cried out in surprise and whirled upon the boulders.

Another shot echoed through the valley and Jim pitched down on his face, making no effort at all to save himself.

From the boulders came Tyler's command, "Ride, you damned fool!"

Lance's quirt cracked and the Spanish spurs dug deep. Bullets sang about him from the riders who drew close behind. The startled horse reared and then leveled out in swift flight.

As he passed the boulders, Tyler swung out of the darkness, half mounted on the running mustang. As he settled himself into the saddle he took a backward shot at the string of men who poured up the trail.

Side by side, Lance and Tyler raced down the length of the pass.

"That was close," shouted Lance. "Thanks."

"I saw your signal," said Tyler. "And boy, when you make signals, you don't stint yourself none."

The running legs of their horses carried them into the spreading blackness of the night. Time after time the darkness behind them was lit by the flash of a revolver. Bullets sang off the blank pass walls and screamed up toward the stars.

They went on, silent now in their determination. Three miles of pass slowly reeled off and they were again in open country, plunging perilously down a mountain slope, tripping and swerving away from abruptly looming obstacles.

And then Tyler pulled in and listened.

"They've lost us," he announced.

"It's about time. This cayuse is about foundered."

"What did you learn down there, pardner?"

Lance looked back at the ragged silhouettes of the range. "He's got fifty men and the place couldn't be cracked by an army. But he's sending a trail herd north in a couple days. Twenty men are going with it, I hear."

"Shore, and that leaves only about thirty for the two of us. Got any ideas?"

"None."

"Huh, neither have I. But doggoned if they can ship my pore cows out of their home like that. It's plumb cruel. The Baron figure to make a fast cleaning?"

"That's what I understand, and there's nothing to stop him. He'll have this range stripped in a couple weeks."

"Won't do no good to send word north. Cows is cows up there. And won't do no good to send word to Santos. Anything we say'd be poison to their ears."

"We ought to do something. You've got me weepin' salt tears about them poor cows of yours."

"Uh-huh, and I reckon Coyote River'll run torrents before I ever see them again. And they was such nice cows too. Big, soulful eyes, with lovin' dispositions. And they liked family life. Never see such affection for one another. And they used to beller plaintively whenever I'd come around. I'll tell a man, pardner, we've got to do something about my pore cows."

Once they heard hoofbeats far to the right and they dismounted to render themselves more invisible. Lance gripped the sticky butt of his Colt, expecting to shoot it out after all. But the noise died.

"They couldn't find a mustang in a corral," said Tyler. "You got any ideas, yet?"

"We might head off the trail herd when it goes out. That'd slow things up considerable."

"Won't do no good. It's things like this that hold up Arizony from becomin' a state like people want. Look at Nevada, for instance. Been a state for years. Look at Texas. Been twenty-five years since they was admitted to the Union. But Arizony..."

"Look what's happened every time they've tried. Some wise yahoos go up to Prescott and say they want us to be a state and then put a lot of things in our constitution a goat couldn't digest. About time somebody did something about it. We ain't even got good cavalry, not blamin' Anderson none.

"Time somebody did something when fellers like the Baron come in and walk off with my pore cows. I got half a notion to send Washington a telegram about it."

"That wouldn't do any good," said Lance, practically. "I was in Washington once and all they got is a lot of shorthorns walkin' around in high hats with big words in their mouths. You got to know somebody to get anything in Washington."

"Well, I know Sam Thorpe. He was out here for a couple years when they sent that crowd of pilgrims to Prescott to govern us. Never see such a thing. They sent them fellers out bag and baggage, territorial government complete, and you know something? Not one of them gents could stick a bronc. And they rode bouncin' up and down and tried to tell us that was the style. Said it was park walkin', or maybe postin', but that didn't take me in. I spent my whole life tryin' to keep daylight from showin' between me and the saddle, and then when they can't, they tell us it's the style. Yah!"

"What about this Sam Thorpe?"

"He was a kind of judge or something, but he wasn't a bad feller. He wanted to see the territory and so I showed him what I could of it. But hell, we'd only been out a month and we couldn't see more'n one section and he wouldn't believe he hadn't seen it all. Guess it's so big he got tired lookin' at it. He came from a shorthorn state named Rhode Island. And Rhode Island, they tell me, has been a state for years and, hell, we're bigger'n six hundred Rhode Islands."

"What's this gent Thorpe now?"

"I dunno. I haven't heard from him for goin' on a year. But the last time he said he was something-something to the secretary of war, or maybe it was something else. General or something."

"Maybe it was an attorney general."

Hoofs clinked to their left and again they sat up, guns in hand, looking intently through the curtain of night. But soon the sound faded.

"Yep," said Tyler. "That's right. Attorney general. But when a man's an assistant to a secretary, he ain't much. I borrowed Slim Johnson's dictionary and looked it up and it said a secretary is a feller that writes letters for somebody else. That don't make Sam very much, does it."

"Wouldn't seem so," said Lance. "I ain't got much of an idea about it, but it seems to me that the attorney general has charge of justice."

"Some kind of a judge, huh?"

"That's right. Must be a soft job, judgin' those slick-ears in the East. They never do nothin'."

Tyler spun his Colts idly, thinking hard. "Maybe if I telegraphed Sam Thorpe he might do something about the Baron takin' all these cows up north. I dunno. You know, we got a railroad into Santos now. That's how they got word about you so fast. Supposin' we just mosey down there and send Sam Thorpe a telegram. I always wanted to send one of the blamed things, but I never had nobody to send one to."

They sat still for an hour but evidently the Baron's men had tired of the search. Finally they mounted their horses and picked their way down to the Coyote River.

"We won't let Brant or Anderson see us," said Tyler. "They don't seem to appreciate our efforts at civic betterment.

They told me they'd hang me if they saw me again and I guess they meant it. Trouble is, I took too much off'n them at poker the other night and they're itchin' for my scalp."

They rode silently after that, threading down the trail which skirted the bases of great, sheer-walled mesas and rock pinnacles which jutted out of the sand to black height against the stars.

Soon they picked up the lights of Santos, but Santos was still three hours' ride away. As they approached there was no greater brilliance to the yellow sparks. They seemed to be standing still.

A train whistled, a foreign sound to this expanse. Tyler turned to Lance. "Hear that? Who says we ain't gettin' fancied up. That's a real, honest-to-God train."

The lights in the coaches strung out, moving slowly in the distance. The train whistled again and, after being in sight for two hours, melted into the blue darkness of the west.

At the outskirts of Santos, Lance and Tyler climbed down and tied their horses to a clump of brush.

"This is going to be risky," said Lance. "Somebody may be hanging around the station."

"Mebbe," grunted Tyler.

Spurs tinkling musically on the platform, they went up to the lighted office. They did not stop at the wicket; they pushed open the door and strode into the room.

The operator glanced up at them through his green eyeshade and took a tuck in his black sleeve guards. He moved nervously back when he saw that both Tyler and Lance held drawn guns.

"Can you send a message to Washington on that thing?" said Tyler.

"Why, yes, of course I can," replied the scared operator, slightly easier when he understood that this was not a holdup.

"Can you write, pardner?" said Tyler to Lance.

"Yep," said Lance and drew a pencil and pad toward him.

"All right," said Tyler, "take this: 'To Sam Thorpe, secretary to the secretary of the Attorney General, Washington, DC.' Got that? All right. 'Dear Sam, I been pretty good lately, how's yourself?' Uh-huh, got that? 'But I've had me a pretty hard time with a feller known as the Baron, seein' that he went and took most of my cows and didn't leave me nothin' to do. So, time bein' heavy on my hands, I'm layin' off to fill this buzzard full of lead. He took most of the cows around here and he's goin' to ship them out north in a couple days and I thought maybe you could have him headed off.' Let's see, got that?

"'It's fellers like this Baron that give Arizony a bad name and lawful hombres like me don't stand a chance havin' only one gun while the Baron's got fifty or so workin' for him.'"

"Wait a minute," said Lance, taut with listening.

From the other end of the platform came the jar of boots. Men were talking and coming closer.

"Troopers," whispered Lance, reaching hastily for the light.

But before he could turn out the yellow glare, two faces appeared on the other side of the wicket. In that instant Lance recognized two of the guards who had once tried to get him. The next instant the room was in darkness.

With a yell, the troopers sped back toward the town.

Citizens turned out of their doorways, loading their guns. Brant bolted from the saloon. Anderson appeared on the general store porch.

A shot rapped into the side of the flimsy building. The operator ducked under the desk.

Tyler kicked the door shut and locked it. Lance took a post beside the window, gun in hand.

"You get back to that blank," said Tyler. "I never sent no telegram before and I ain't goin' to let these ignorant, mule-faced mavericks stop me now."

Tyler fired through a hole in the glass, sighted carefully and fired again. Lance seated himself at the table and took up the pencil.

"It's hard to write in the dark," said Lance, "but fire away."

"Got what I said? All right. 'It ain't easy for us to stop this Baron because there ain't nobody but a couple troops of cavalry here and they ain't enough to do anything.'" His heavy Colts roared again and he grunted that he had missed. "'But I ain't able to do anything here in Santos because the citizens are sort of set agin' me, besides naturally bein' given to argument.

"'There's a young feller workin' with me named Lance Gordon that's a pretty good gent and a public benefactor, havin' eliminated some of the bad element over in Los Gatos already, showin' that he dotes on civic duty. But we can't . . .'" He depressed the muzzle of his Colt and fired. "Missed him. No I didn't, I hit his arm. All right, you got that?

"As I was sayin', 'It's things like this that gives Arizony a bad name and I think you ought to tell the President to maybe do something about stoppin' the Baron from shippin' my cows and everybody else's up to the north, that bein' classed as stealin' here, same as anyplace else.

"'My health . . .'" A bullet slapped through the window, showering the room with glass. Yells came up from all sides. "'My health,'" said Tyler, "'is pretty good so far and I hope nobody's been stealin' your cows like they have mine. And don't forget to tell the President to do something about the Baron, him bein' an ornery, lowdown longhorn that don't deserve to live. Meanin' the Baron, not the President. Very truly yours, M. R. Tyler.' Got that? Then c'mon up here and help me stand these lobos off."

Lance went to the window on the other side and peered cautiously forth. Men were creeping up under the cover of the platform edge. He took three quick shots at their coat tails, the only visible part, and sent them skittering back across the tracks.

A voice bawled at them from outside, "If you give up peaceful-like, we'll give you a fair trial."

"That's Brant," said Tyler, shooting toward the sound.

"Wonder when the troopers'll get here," said Lance.

"'Most any minute," said Tyler. He pulled the operator out from under the table and plunked him down before the telegraph key, tossing the message at him.

"You get that off, pronto," said Tyler. "I want to be sure it goes."

The operator's shaking hand went to the switches and he began to clear the line. He took the roughly written sheets and although he added an unnecessary number of dots here and there, he began to send.

Lance moved to another window and saw that three men were trying to advance under the cover of a baggage truck. He caromed bullets off the steel bracing and the truck was hastily deserted.

"Good thing it's dark," said Lance.

"Yep," said Tyler, across the room.

The clicking key sounded puny in the crash of Colts, but it went on fast enough.

"Wonder how we'll get out of here," said Tyler.

Lance went into the baggage room and saw that two barrels of whiskey had come on the last train, destined for the Diamond Palace Saloon. With a strength lent by the necessity for haste, he knocked out the tops with his gun butt and opened a small trap in the center of the floor.

Then with rapid motions and with a fine disregard for the whiskey, he poured both barrels through the trap. The fluid ran with a gay gurgle, sending fumes boiling about the room. Then he went to the office again.

"S'time we did something, Tyler," said Lance. "Look here, operator, you all through with that?"

A shot showered splinters from the wall over the operator's head. He dived hastily under the desk again and peered cautiously up at Lance. "Y-Y-Yessir."

"Then listen, we're goin' to be in those barrels, and if they ask you what happened to us, you tell 'em we escaped five minutes ago in the darkness and headed south. Got it? If you

39

don't, then I'll plug you through a bunghole. And remember, I'll be seeing you down my sights."

"Y-Y-Y-Yessir!"

"C'mon, Tyler."

Tyler grinned through his beard. "It's gonna be close quarters, but the perfume's mighty nice."

Lance upended a barrel over Tyler's head and then one over his own. When he settled himself, Lance had a clear view of the office through the bunghole he had knocked out.

For several minutes the shooting kept up outside and then, when nothing answered their lead, the citizens of Santos grew more bold, especially when the two troops of cavalry came up from the fort.

Suddenly the door splintered open and Anderson tramped into the room, looking very mad and holding a revolver as though anxious to use it. He stared about him and then called to Brant and the others. When the sheriff came, the operator edged cautiously out from under the desk. They seized him by the shirt and shook him.

The operator tried hard to keep his gaze off the barrels visible through the door of the baggage room. "Th-th-they left about five minutes ago. Th-th-th-they went south."

"You had that end, you fool!" Anderson bellowed at Brant. "And you let 'em slip through."

Brant, anxious to redeem himself, rushed out of the door shouting, "Get your horses. We'll catch 'em before they hit the border!"

The room was cleared and soon hoofbeats thundered away into the south.

Lance shoved the barrel off his head. The fumes of the whiskey had made him groggy. His clothing reeked of liquor. He lifted the barrel off Tyler, but Tyler sat where he was.

"Don't disturb me," said Tyler, blissfully, eyes closed. "I never knew you could get soused just breathin' the stuff."

CHAPTER FIVE

Stampede

THREE days later Lance and Tyler were still camped beside the dry bed of the Coyote River. It was night and the plain glowed beneath a slice of moon.

Tyler leaned against a rock pulling on a carefully cupped cigarette. "See anything yet?"

Lance was laying along the top of a rock, Sharps rifle at his side, looking toward the mouth of the pass. "Nothing at all. I figure if they're going to start that drive they'd have done it before now."

"Seems as how," said Tyler, "the Baron has given us the go-by. Funny, but there ain't any other way out of the basin and we haven't stopped lookin' all this whole time. Grub's almost gone, too. Maybe we better go back to Santos and break into the general store again. It's moonlight and maybe we could see good enough not to get hold of such moldy sowbelly like we did last time."

"He couldn't have gotten out and that means he's still in. And I'm not ridin' down that pass, Tyler. No way out and he'll have guards strung all along it since I escaped."

"It's moonlight," said Tyler. "Maybe if we went up to that pinnacle of rock over there we could take a look. No use one of us stayin' here."

"I'll stay and if they come out, I'll stampede 'em back in like we planned."

"By yourself? Needs two of us. One to take care of the advance riders. I keep thinkin' how swell it would be if the Baron and the whole crew tailed the herd. If they all got caught in there and we stampeded the whole herd back at 'em . . . That's shore a sight I want to see. He ain't goin' to part me and my pore cows if I can help it."

"Well, let's both of us go, then. We could see if there were any left in the basin anyhow. If there ain't, then he's slipped out another way and we've been coolin' our heels for three days for nothin'."

Tyler got up and began to take in on his mount's stake rope. Lance slid off the rock and saddled his own horse.

"There's one place," said Tyler, "we can get down into the pass, but we can't get back up without a derrick. You come over from that pinnacle and hit the pass square in the middle along a ridge. That's how I got there the night they chased you out. Maybe if we hit there we wouldn't find no guards."

"The guards are further in," said Lance.

They forked their broncs and rode at a walk toward the finger of rock which pointed up at the moon. The plains were spooky and their mounts shied at the shadowy, crouching clumps of brush.

"Maybe we hadn't ought to leave," said Tyler, "but I'm gettin' terrible tired of waitin'. And besides I hone to see them critters of mine."

Lance paused to listen occasionally, half expecting to trip

across the Baron's scouts. They were on the north side of the basin, on very dangerous ground.

But they arrived without mishap at the pinnacle and dismounted. Tyler led the way up the path toward the summit, clinging to small clumps of grass to steady himself.

At the top all the plains were spread out for their study and the silvered world was brilliant in the half-light.

Lance stared intently down into the basin and swore. "He's given us the slip!"

"By God, you're right! It's empty."

"Well, if this don't beat—Wait a minute, Tyler. What's that shadow movin' over there? Looks like a cloud runnin' along the ground."

Tyler peered intently for a full minute and then cried, "It's the herd! It's the herd! Well, damn my eyes, he's movin' out. Oh lord, we waited for three days and then when he moves out . . ."

Lance wasn't waiting for any further word. He plunged down the steep trail, high-heel boots barely holding to the earth, spurs catching in the clumps of grass.

Tyler scrambled after him. "Hey, don't kill yourself. There ain't any use now. We can't get ahead of them in time and if we stampede 'em on the plains, they'll kill us and just gather 'em up again. Hey, Lance. Wait for me!"

Lance mounted on the run, his wild-eyed bronc rearing. Lance waited impatiently until Tyler crawled his horse.

"Lead off for that pass center," said Lance. "We can follow them anyhow."

"Ornery, murderin' lobo," said Tyler, applying quirt and spur. "He would have to do that. Just as if he knowed where we was all the time."

They rode recklessly over the short distance, risking spills in dry washes, plunging toward the ridge. Lance realized then what a wild ride Tyler must have made to save him that night and he experienced a warm wave of appreciation.

The herd was filing out of the pass mouth long before they reached the center, but Tyler and Lance had hopes that they could do something.

They arrived at the one middle pass entrance without regard to the noise they made. It was impossible to hear above the thunder of split hoofs and the lowing of the cattle on the move. Dust was choking, blotting out the moon. Cattle were packed half the length of the pass.

Tyler looked into the split, "The rear guard's just passin'."

"Let's get down," cried Lance, dismounting and swinging over the edge. "If we trail them, maybe we can start a stampede anyway and cause a heap of trouble."

"Don't run into that guard, you fool! There's forty men down there!"

Lance held back until the loafing ponies had gone by and then he began to drop ten feet at a time down the sheer wall. Tyler dropped a lariat to help him and quickly followed.

When they reached the pass floor, invisible in the fog of dust, Lance said, "I wonder where the Baron is."

"Probably up front where the dust ain't so bad. What'll we do for horses now? The other time I jumped mine down and damn near broke his legs. Maybe I ought to go back up . . ."

"Here's our horses," said Lance, climbing up on a boulder the height of a man.

Two punchers, evidently the last of the herd's rear guard, came slowly riding through the dust, neckerchiefs tied across their faces.

Lance did not wait to see if Tyler was there. He launched himself at the first man, straight as an arrow, clubbed .45 in hand. He struck and clutched the horn. The puncher weaved drunkenly in the saddle.

A sharp cry and a grunt came above the rumble of the herd and Lance knew that Tyler had gotten his man. Lance lifted the puncher he had knocked out and laid him across the rock.

Tyler saw the movement and put his man across the other. Then, as though nothing had happened, Tyler and Lance began to ride out after the rear guard, faces hidden beneath the protection of their bandanas.

"Wait until they hit the plains," said Tyler. "Then we'll start shooting and spread them cows all over the range. And maybe in the confusion, we can knock off the Baron, damn him."

But whatever their plans, they would not be executed that night. The tone of the herd changed. The bawling cattle began to bunch up. The thunder was deafening and growing louder.

"What the hell," said Lance. "Maybe they struck a snag."

He and Tyler reined in and sat listening. The roar grew louder and louder until it almost split their eardrums.

Suddenly a man whipped down the pass toward them, a gray spectre out of the dust. "Run, you fools!" he yelped.

Lance and Tyler wheeled their mounts uncertainly and stared after him.

"He looked like he was goin' someplace," said Tyler.

"In a hurry," agreed Lance.

Three riders materialized out of the darkness and, with whips cracking, sped back toward the basin, almost running down the two who stood in the pass.

"Run!" bellowed the fellow in the lead.

"Now what the hell do you suppose . . ." began Tyler.

The lowing of crazed cattle, the click and snap of horn against horn, the roll of thousands of hoofs shook the world.

Five riders whipped down the pass, wild-eyed with fear.

"Stampede!" squalled the man in the lead.

"Oh, my gawd," said Tyler, "they're running at us!"

They wheeled but the horses needed no coaxing. The ponies knew cattle too well to loiter. Something had frightened the skittish herd at the pass entrance and the cattle had turned back into the basin.

"We'll be caught in here!" yelled Lance, but the roar drowned his words.

They were in the midst of a tight press of men and horses, all of them with but one thought—to get back into the basin ahead of the stampede, to get out of the juggernaut's way.

Beside Lance a horse stumbled and went down, throwing the rider into the blur of running, churning hoofs.

It seemed to Lance that the mile and a half back to the basin was ten thousand leagues. Tyler was at his side, forcing his mount to greater effort. Lance's hat whipped off and hung about his neck by the chin thong, choking him, but he could not loosen it.

They were in the midst of a tight press of men and horses, all of them with but one thought—

Horn against horn, thousands of hoofs shaking the world, glaze-eyed, frightened beasts running under a pall of dust which rose up to engulf the moon. No telling what had started them and no man worried now. It was ride and ride hard and you might get out alive if your horse didn't stumble and if your horse was fast enough and if you kept lathered leather between your knees.

Forty riders, Lance and Tyler, fled, fastest horses to the fore. And the beasts Lance and Tyler had acquired were not of the best. Their riders, on top of that boulder in the pass, were safe enough, far safer than their brothers.

"If I ever get out of this," said Lance between set teeth, but not really believing it, "I'll never look at another cow."

CHAPTER SIX

The Fight in the Basin

AHEAD the Coyote River basin spread out before them like a winning hand in a poker game. The riders fanned to the right and left, running down the trail, scattering out over the meadows, getting out of the way of the herd.

And once they were safe, they immediately began to devise ways and means of starting the animals milling.

From the pass there burst the cattle, running with their heads up, bellowing as though pursued by all the fiends in hell. The avalanche of bodies ran like a brown river across the center of the basin toward the other side, following the leaders and the leaders running blind.

Now that the thunder was not pent up in the pass, men could hear themselves.

"Turn them to the right!" bellowed Fallon.

"Turn them to the right!" echoed through the basin.

Lance and Tyler headed for the ranch houses, choosing that place as the best point to defend. They had no illusions about their fate. They were penned up in the basin and they'd never get out alive if they were found. And that they would be found depended only upon the ticking seconds.

Tyler flung himself off his horse and sprinted for the bunkhouse, carrying the rifle he had whisked from the saddle

51

boot and the saddlebags which would contain ammunition. Lance was close behind him, carrying a Sharps.

They slammed the door behind them and in the pale shaft of the dust-dimmed moon, regarded each other.

"You look like an end man in a minstrel show," panted Tyler.

Lance looked at the other's dust-caked face, grinning. "Guess so, and you wouldn't take any beauty prize yourself. That was touch and go for a minute."

"Touch and go is right. I heard angel's wings aflutterin' over my head and Saint Pete was already openin' up his gates, ready to say, 'Hello, Tyler. Git down and come in.'"

"That wasn't Saint Pete," said Lance. "That was a feller with a pitchfork and long horns. Look, they're turnin' 'em."

They both peered through a grimy window and saw that the herd had started to circle, still running but slowing down in bewilderment.

"Wonder what started 'em off."

Lance shook his head. "They was always a spooky bunch. Fast brandin' must have set their nerves on edge. You got plenty of shells for that Henry?"

"Yep."

"Well, get 'em ready. Here comes Fallon."

Tyler shoved the Henry's muzzle out through the window. "That means they won't move 'em again tonight."

"Herd and boys all wore out, I reckon," said Lance. "If they would trail, we wouldn't have to worry."

"Who's worryin'?" said Tyler, squinting down the sights. "Might as well start hostilities now while the startin's good."

Fallon reined in before the corral and looked back at the

men who were calming the cattle. Then he dismounted and strode toward the bunkhouse.

"Wait," said Lance, laying his hand to block the sights. "Let him come in."

Fallon threw back the door and strode into the dim interior. He did not see the two men until Lance spoke.

"Sit down, Fallon," said Lance. "A man owes himself a rest after a ride like that."

Fallon tried to go for his gun, but Lance slammed him back against the wall.

"That ain't exactly healthy, Fallon," said Lance. Working with a broken riata, he trussed Fallon and lugged him to a bunk. Laying him inside, he tucked a ragged blanket under his chin. "Don't mind us," said Lance, "just doze off. You look plumb wore out."

Fallon glared and muttered something vile into his gag. Lance went back to the window. "Wasn't any use givin' ourselves away just yet."

"You're right," said Tyler. "Look, who's that big gent on the black horse? Somebody told me Napoleon looked like that, settin' on a knoll, watchin' a battle."

"That's the Baron," said Lance. "Fancy, ain't he. Wonder if I could dust him a little with this Sharps." He took the heavy, single-shot weapon and adjusted the sights. "Hard to shoot by moonlight. What would you say that range was?"

Tyler pushed Lance's gun muzzle away. "Here, wait a minute yourself. I got me an idea."

Tyler went out of the bunkhouse and mounted Fallon's horse. Then he ran rapidly about the 'dobe three times to attract attention. Finally he paused and looked up at the knoll. He swung his arm in an imperative "come here" signal.

The Baron looked down for several seconds and then, with a glance to make certain that the herd was getting into some sort of shape, started down the hill toward the bunkhouse.

Tyler swung down and strode toward the door, entering.

Presently the Baron got down outside and pushed the door open with his foot.

"Fallon?" said the Baron. "What's the matter . . ."

But the dim shape which moved toward him was not Fallon. The Baron yelled, whipped a gun from his shoulder holster and, before Lance could strike it down, fired hastily.

Lance came up from his crouch and sent a hard fist into the Baron's jaw. The short gun went spinning.

"Hey!" cried Tyler. "They're coming!" He started to leave the window and join in the fight, but he turned back and fired at a horseman who had popped up on the other side of the corral. Once more he tried to break away, but three men were coming. He jacked another shell into the Henry and fired a second time.

The Baron braced himself and jumped to the attack. Lance had not drawn before and there was no time now. Lance met the Baron's rush with a well-timed left which sent the bigger man skidding into the table. The table spread its legs and went down.

Lance launched himself across the room, but the Baron was up before he could get there. They stood firmly in the center of the floor, slugging as men slug when they are used to the quicker defense of powder smoke.

"Finish him," begged Tyler from the window. "They're surroundin' us!" Again he tried to find time to stop the fight, but the sudden appearance of a man directly before the 'dobe brought him again to the window and the Henry.

Lance set himself. The Baron charged. Lance brought all his weight into one blow. The Baron met it with his chin and staggered back, his arms going like a windmill. He struck the bunks with his head and rebounded into a savage chest blow.

The Baron went down, limply and finally. With a softly spoken word of thanks, Lance picked up the rest of the riata and hogtied the unconscious man. Fallon writhed in the bunk.

"You take the other side," cried Tyler. "I got my tally here, but they don't know enough to go and hide."

Lance cocked his .45 and thrust it through the window. A bullet snapped eagerly beside his ear.

"It's that feller said he was Windy Green!" came a cry from without.

"Get him!" cried another.

"It'll be up in two minutes," said Tyler. "These gents is killers."

Lance was finding that out. A steady volleying from the shadows of other 'dobes and from a ramshackle hay barn made his position untenable. His face was gashed with flying splinters. A chip was gone from his ear and his collar stuck to the back of his neck.

But he managed to get in a few shots. A gunslinger spilled out of cover, his hat rolling away from him and his arms flopping out as though to retrieve it. Another rolled limply from the hay barn loft.

"Look at the powder they're wastin'," jeered Tyler, from across the room.

A group of men formed to charge the door, suddenly remembering that from that side there were no loopholes.

"It's all up," said Lance. "S'long, Tyler."

"S'long, pardner. Too bad we didn't get elected to Congress."

The firing outside doubled, trebled, as though the men were trying to cover the attack.

Abruptly bullets stopped whacking through the room. Tyler and Lance, braced for one final stand, were mystified.

"Don't that beat hell?" said Tyler.

"What's happening out there?"

Men were running out of cover and heading for the other 'dobes. Lance crossed the room to Tyler's side, watching.

"Didn't know we was that dangerous," said Tyler.

"No use lettin' 'em go in there," said Lance. He fired swiftly at the door of the other 'dobe and the men stumbled over the body of the first one to enter. The crowd turned back in haste and tried to dive to other shelter.

And then horses and riders came out of nowhere and things moved so fast that no man could tell what was happening.

Lance and Tyler felt like actors who have had the show stolen from them. But they pegged relentlessly at the Baron's men who still scurried about.

The moonlight struck through the dust and lit up brass buttons and gleaming sabers. Anderson swept like a mounted whirlwind through the fray, revolver cracking.

"The cavalry," said Lance in wonder.

"And there's Brant," cried Tyler. "Maybe I better plug him now before he makes trouble for us."

"He won't make any trouble for us," said Lance. "Hell, man, we're heroes, get it? We're the fellers that stood off the whole gang and made this possible."

Things had quieted outside and Lance and Tyler thought the opportunity to show themselves had come. They stepped out of the 'dobe and walked up to Anderson, smiling at the officer and quite ready to receive praise.

"There they are!" somebody sang out.

Anderson wheeled his horse and brought up his revolver. "Stand where you are, men."

"Wait a minute," said Tyler. "We done all this. We got the Baron and Fallon in there for you, all tied up."

"Get in there," barked Anderson to a pair of troopers. And to Brant and some more of his men he said, "Take these two men and herd them with the rest."

"Wait a minute," said Tyler. "You can't do this. Lance and me have been fighting this here gang and we saved you a lot of trouble. Ain't you got no gratitude?"

"I know nothing about that," said Anderson. "You men are under arrest and you'll probably hang. You know you killed two men when you raided Santos?"

"Two men?" said Lance. "Raided Santos? You're crazy as a strychnined wolf. We didn't raid Santos. We went there to send a telegram. Any law against sendin' a telegram?"

"You killed two men," repeated Anderson. "Get over there or I'll drill you."

The two troopers came out with the Baron and Fallon and Anderson's attention was diverted to them.

The Baron looked very rumpled and crestfallen. Fallon cringed.

"I've got orders to place you men under arrest," said Anderson. "They'll try you at Prescott and hang you. Those were the orders I received."

It was a dreary cavalcade that moved out of the basin under the moon. Men were holding the cattle for future reference, men from Santos.

"An' I lose my cows again," mourned Tyler, riding with hands firmly tied to his pommel.

Lance nodded. "Looks like there's more'n two troops here."

"Uh-huh, some of these soldiers are down from Flagstaff, I reckon. Wonder how come they got down from there."

"I dunno," said Lance, miserably. "You don't suppose when Anderson really understands that we did him a good turn . . ."

"Not a chance. I can tell he's acting under military orders, and he shore can be military when he's away from a faro table."

"Silence back there," barked a sergeant.

And with the other prisoners, the Baron among them, Lance and Tyler silently finished the ride back across the Coyote River and to Santos.

A cheering populace met them. But the citizens of Santos barely knew the Baron and had not even seen the gunslingers from other ranges before. The citizens of Santos spotted Lance Gordon and Tyler and the shouts which came from the high walks were depressing.

"So you will raid Santos!"

"There they go, the murderers."

"They don't look so pert now, do they?"

"We'll string 'em up!"

"Looks like they're sore at us," said Tyler, dolefully. "We didn't do nothin'."

They progressed the length of the street with the cavalry flanking them. Lance decided he had never seen a dawn so bleak and cold.

"It's all up," mourned Tyler. "And I'll never get another look at them pore cows. Wonder if they'll use a firing squad."

They knew then that Anderson was merely parading them. The arrogant gunfighters exchanged glare for glare with the citizens and troopers. The Baron rode between the blue files with his head on his chest.

Anderson held up his hand and stopped. He was abreast of the railway station and he could not resist a bit of showmanship for the town, which came closer to hear what he would say.

The operator came out at Anderson's signal and started to say something but Anderson silenced him.

"Get me a blank," said Anderson.

The operator went back and got the blank and when he came out again he looked down the line toward Tyler and Lance Gordon. His eyes opened up a little and he smiled.

"The son . . ." muttered Tyler.

"Captain . . ." began the operator.

But Anderson was going to do the talking. "Send this message to the War Department, Washington, DC. That's right. Now write, 'Beg to report that man known as Baron and gang have been put down and arrested. The Baron is now in custody with his men. Have also arrested notorious gunman named Lance Gordon and a bandit named Tyler.'"

"Pardon me, sir," said a lieutenant Santos did not know. "Aren't you going to give the Flagstaff men any credit at all?"

"Oh, certainly," said Anderson with a smile. "Operator, add, 'Raid was ably assisted by presence of Troops A and B from Flagstaff garrison.'"

"That means a firing squad for us," said Tyler, whispering. "Under territorial and military law, we're practically in the army now."

In spite of the fact that he should not keep his tired men waiting, in answer to questions from the townsmen, Anderson leaned forward in his saddle, gauntleted hand poised on his saber hilt.

"Oh, it was a brisk enough fight," said Anderson. "We met the advance guard, surrounded them and took them, but the firing started a stampede of the cattle back through the pass. Then we rode after the herd, surrounded the main gang and shot it out with them. No, we only had one man wounded. Lucky, eh?"

"Lucky, hell," said Tyler in a loud voice. "We had the whole outfit jumping when you got there."

Anderson glared and a trooper prodded Tyler with a revolver.

"It'll come out at the trial," said Lance. "Tyler and I were trying . . ."

Another revolver prodded Lance.

"We'd better move along," said Anderson, nervously.

"Wait a minute, sir," said the telegraph operator. "I had a message for Tyler. I tried to tell you . . ."

"Prisoners cannot receive messages," said Anderson.

Curiosity of Santos overrode Anderson's order.

"Let's see what's in it," chorused the men along the platform.

The operator smiled at Anderson, evidently enjoying a joke of his own and passed the message over to Tyler. As operator, he knew what it said. A trooper unlashed Tyler's hands.

Tyler read the operator's precise handwriting and then read it again. He swore and read it a third time.

"What's it say?" said Lance.

Tyler sat up importantly in spite of the warning revolver which pointed at him meaningly now that his hands were loose.

"It says," said Tyler, stifling a laugh, "it says: 'M. R. Tyler, Santos, Territory of Arizona. This will advise you of your appointment as United States Deputy Marshal at large in Arizona Territory and will also advise Mr. Lance Gordon of a like appointment. I have advised the Attorney General of your sterling character and he acted upon my recommendation immediately. Confirming papers will follow by mail. Your first task is to act with the cavalry the Secretary of War is sending from Flagstaff. The matter of the Baron of course is part of your new duties. Officials at Prescott have been advised. Sam Thorpe, Asst. Atty. Gen.' "

Anderson was so astounded he removed his hand from his sword hilt. "But that can't take effect. You . . . you haven't your badge of office. . . ."

"And I don't need none," said Tyler. "My badge is in the mail and this appointment is dated three days ago, or two anyway."

"Then," said Anderson, "you disgraced your office by raiding Santos and you therefore forfeit your badge."

"I did not," said Tyler. "We wasn't United States Deputy Marshals then. This appointment came afterwards. I know my law, I do."

"Take off these ropes," ordered Lance.

And when the ropes were stripped away, Lance reined his mount out from the file, moving beside Tyler.

"Captain," said Tyler, "you done a pretty good job for a soldier, bringin' the prisoners in for us this way. Course we had them all rounded up first. You can give us a hand keepin' 'em for the general hangin' if you want. I'll get us a United States district attorney down here to try 'em, this bein' a territory and their act therefore a federal crime, so to speak."

Anderson glared, but he nevertheless reined back.

"But," said Anderson, "Gordon killed a deputy marshal in Los Gatos. He's got to stand trial for that."

"Hell no," said Tyler. "The Department of Justice just lost one and had to replace him, didn't they? And Lance is quicker on the gun than MacLeod was. So they just wanted the fastest they could get on the draw and the test proved it. And if he does have to stand trial, this'll fix it up, what he did tonight."

Anderson could not answer that and Tyler winked broadly at Lance and reached down, taking the telegram Anderson had written out of the operator's hand.

"Take another one, son," said Tyler. "'To the Department of Justice, Washington, DC. Have got the Baron ready for the calaboose and the rope. Shoot a district attorney down here for a fast trial as the citizens is itchin' for a lynchin'. We had a pretty tough scrap and neither Deputy Marshal Gordon or myself got hurt, only some outlaws. The cavalry came around soon enough to get a trooper wounded by a stray bullet but otherwise did no damage. Thanks for the appointment and regards to the President, United States Deputy Marshal M. R. Tyler, Santos, Arizony Territory. And PS I hope this appointment don't keep me from havin' no cows because my pardner and myself have got about eight thousand head we'd like to grab hold of up near Coyote River.'"

Tyler beamed at Lance and Lance beamed at Tyler and together they beamed at Anderson. The citizens cheered, eager to be on the side of the new law, and everybody but maybe Anderson and the Baron were happy.

"Captain," said Tyler, "you take these gents and hold them for a spell. Me, I got to get some breakfast. C'mon, Lance."

Reign of the Gila Monster

Reign of the Gila Monster

YOU heard me!" bawled Howdy Johnson, banging his fist on the bar so hard that glasses rattled in every one of Ringtail's six saloons. "You can't deny it! You know doggone well that Powderville is the roughest, toughest, fightingest, rooty-tootin' six-gun-shootin' cow town on the whole blamed trail!"

"I ain't said nothin' to the contrary," pleaded the ruddy-faced barkeep timidly.

"You did!" contradicted Howdy. "You did so! You said that Ringtail was wild. I heard you with my own ears, I did. And there ain't any man this side of Laredo that can stand right in front of me and malign my town like that. You know Powderville is wild. You heard all about Powderville.

"Ringtail, bah! What's Ringtail? A collection of tombstones, that's what. A collection of skeletons. The only reason they laid it out was to bury it. You ain't had a killin' in this town for three days. You ain't had to order a new bar mirror for a month. I'm s'prised you don't peddle skim milk."

"I just said—" bleated the barkeep.

"Oh, so I'm a liar, am I? You tryin' to run down Powderville, are you? Well listen, mister. In the past eight months I been to Chicago, see? I been in every town from Powderville to

Chicago. And what do I find? A lot of tame goats, that's what. Ringtail couldn't stand up two minutes against Powderville. Not one minute! Powderville is tough. There ain't nobody in that town that ain't a hard case. They're a nest of sidewinders, that's what. Loud? You can hear 'em all the way to El Paso on a clear night."

The barkeep ventured, "You . . . ah . . . must be from Powderville, mister."

"From Powderville?" shouted Howdy. "I'll say I'm from Powderville. And not only that, I founded Powderville. I'm one of the city fathers, I am. I'm the gent that walked in there and I said, 'Right here we're going to put a town, and it's going to be the roughest, toughest, fightingest town—'"

A hand fell on Howdy's shoulder. A consoling hand. Howdy turned to confront a sad-eyed, flop-eared, hang-jowled gentleman of travel-worn aspect.

"Goood gosh!" yipped Howdy. "If it ain't Poison Peters. Man alive, you sure are a sight for sore eyes! I been to hell and back. I been all the way to Chi and I ain't had airy a good time for eight long months. By God, it's sure dandy to see you, Poison. You'n me can ride back to Powderville and when we get there, I'll buy out every drop in your mangy old saloon and—"

"The saloon ain't no more," said Poison Peters, choking up with emotion.

"What? You mean they ain't no more Bucket-o'-Blood Saloon? What's the matter, burn down?"

"No," said Poison Peters, struggling to down his sobs.

"Tornado hit the place?"

"No," gulped Poison, swabbing at his whiskery face with a dirty hand back.

"Did they break you up complete?" cried the astounded Howdy.

"It . . . it ain't that," wept Poison. "It's . . . it's the Gila Monster."

"What kind of trash you talking about?" barked Howdy.

"It ain't no trash. It's the truth. Look here, Howdy."

They went to the door and there in the dust of Ringtail was a wagon. On it rested a shattered mirror, a mahogany bar, three barrels of whiskey and several hampers of glasses. A bung starter protruded from under the box, a scatter-gun lay upon the seat. Over all lay a sign on which was scrawled, "Bucket-o'-Blood Saloon. Powderville's Roughest, Toughest—" The last two words were completely blotted out. It was even hard to read "Roughest" and "Toughest."

Slack-jawed, Howdy turned to Poison and stammered, "But-but what happened? Did-did business get bad or—"

"Gone to hell," blubbered Poison.

"No more trail herds, maybe?" prompted Howdy.

"Lots of trail herds. D-D-Don't make me go on, Howdy. I can't stand to talk about it, it's that awful."

"But look here," yelled Howdy. "You can't just up and quit like that. Goood gosh! You was heart and soul of the town. You can't quit. Ain't you got no civic pride? We worked for two years to make Powderville the Mecca of the trail and now you pull out just as though everybody'd died."

"It ain't that," mourned Poison. "It's the Gila Monster. It's awful, Howdy. It's horrible. I can't bear to talk about it."

"Well, for gosh sakes, who's the Gila Monster? What kind of hogwash is that?"

"He's a man. He come into Powderville five, six months ago. Name of Gilman. Big gent—seven feet two. Shoulders like a hogshead. Face like pounded steak. He's tough. He's so good with a Peacemaker he can throw up a dime and hit it six times before it lights. He's so hard you'd bend a nail if you tried to drive one into him. He spit at a tarantula and the thing went blind. He bites spikes in half. He can bend a shotgun barrel in one hand."

"But," protested Howdy, "that's the kind of gent we want in Powderville. Don't tell me he didn't enter into the spirit of the thing. Why didn't you talk to him and give him some civic pride?"

"I did. I must have talked too much. I gave him lots of civic pride and the first thing you know, he went and appointed himself town marshal. He says it's high time we reformed. He don't allow drinkin' after six o'clock. No gamblin'. Nobody in town can wear iron but him. Absolutely no killin' allowed, no matter what you think of the other gent. And say, you don't dast spit lessen he fines you for it. He says we all got to levy taxes or something, and so he collects ten dollars a day from every man that wants to stay in the town, and he killed four fellers dead when they refused to pay it. Tax on a saloon is fifty dollars a day. I tell you, Howdy, it breaks me all up just to think about it."

"Why didn't somebody plug him?"

"Two gents tried it and we had to pass the hat to bury 'em.

70

I tell you he's a panther ridin' forked lightning. Don't you go down there, Howdy."

"Why not? Ain't I as good as he is?"

"No," sobbed Poison.

"I'm mad," stated Howdy. "Here I been countin' on havin' a good old time in Powderville and I come back to find out that everything has gone to hell for keeps. Well, let me tell you this, Poison, you may be lacking in civic pride, but I ain't. No, sir! Ain't no man livin' goin' to state that Howdy Johnson turned his back on his town. I'm goin' down there and—"

"Please," begged Poison. "Stay out of Powderville, Howdy. You got a wild reputation and if you show your face down there, he'll shoot you down just like that. You wasn't never known as a good gunman, Howdy—"

"What? What the hell do you think I been doing for eight months, knitting? You don't know what I been up to. You ain't got the faintest idea what I been up to. No, sir. Look here, Poison. I'm touched. I'm affected. There ain't nothing like this going to happen to my hometown. This is the time for action. This is the moment to blow 'charge.'"

"You mean taps," gulped Poison. "No use, Howdy. You play safe. We'll start another town an'—"

"Never! My heart is plumb set on Powderville. You goin' to let just one lone gunman run you out of there? No! These gunmen are all yellah. Every one of them is yellah. I—"

"Not the Gila Monster. Not Gilman. He ain't yellah. Nawsir, he'd eat live lions and enjoy it, that gent. You stay out of Pow—"

71

"Never," cried Howdy, striking a haughty pose. "Even Hannibal had his Waterloo, and that goes for the Gila Monster. Turn that wagon, Poison. We're headin' for Powderville right now!"

Poison Peters had not in the least overstated Gilman. When the man sat in his swivel chair and stretched his feet out across the marshal's desk, he came close to filling up the whole building. His hat, on the back of his head, looked bigger than an umbrella, and his guns, lashed down, were only a shade smaller than howitzers.

His boots were so large that he had once stepped on Zeb Chumley's hound dog and fifty witnesses were ready to attest that not even an inch of the animal's tail was visible. The rowels on his spurs bonged like fire bells when he walked and were, in themselves, larger than Mexican dollars. He could take a bottle of whiskey in his hand, close his fingers and say, "Which one have I got it in?"

In short, Gilman, dubbed the Gila Monster, was colossal in size. But his temper was bigger than he was. When he got mad, he spat sparks longer than a bullet could carry. He turned the color of a thundercloud's belly and roared louder than a stampeding herd.

From constant practice, his trigger finger twitched even when he slept, at the rate of five twitches a minute by actual count. And, from habit, every time the finger twitched, his hand threw up as though from a recoil.

He was touchy. He had been known to shoot a man just

because that man brushed against him. He had shot a man for buying him a drink. He had shot a man for not buying.

He had civic pride, he said. He was, he said, a reformer. He was, he said, a lawful citizen bent upon saving Powderville from its vices. He had, everybody said, saved Powderville with a thoroughness which bordered on extinction.

At the moment, he was talking in a mild voice. He could not be heard farther than the city limits. And the dust blown up from his boots and desk was scarcely larger than a tornado's funnel. He was, in fact, in one of his more peaceful moods.

"Just you let any of them gents show up here," said Gilman. "Just you let any one of them poke their nose inside the limits of our beautiful town and zowie! That's the way to do business."

Lippy Connor was standing in the doorway, listening. It was rare for anyone to take a chair in Gilman's office because, in the first place, he never invited them to, and in the second place, getting out of a chair took precious instants.

Lippy beamed flabbily and nodded with sturdy enthusiasm. "You bet," said Lippy gingerly.

"You just let any two of them, any dozen of them, show up in Powderville," said Gilman amiably, "and I'll shoot so many holes in them you could use their hides for windows."

He waved a monstrous paw at the rough plank board on which many reward posters were tacked. It was highly unlikely that most of these advertised gentlemen would show up in Powderville, but Gilman lacked a subject for conversation.

Lippy Connor peered at the designated board and beamed

dutifully. Suddenly the beam stiffened, his jaw slacked, his eyes protruded like green balls in a drugstore window.

"Ain't that Howdy Johnson's name there?" whispered Lippy.

"Howdy Johnson?" snorted Gilman. "Who's Howdy Johnson?"

"Up there on the board," said Lippy, pointing from the door.

"Hmmm, hmmm, hmmm," said Gilman, like a saw hitting a nail. "Tiger Svenson. Black Bug Stewart. Gunner Thompson . . . ah . . . there it is. Howdy Johnson. Yep, there it is. Third from the bottom. Came in just a while back. Says:

"'Howdy Johnson. Wanted Dead or Alive. One thousand five hundred dollars reward. If seen, notify Chicago police and ship body for identification. Five foot ten inches. Stocky build. Unshaven face. Blue eyes with slight squint. Emphatic method of talking. Be careful of this man because he is dangerous. Has killed three police officers in Chicago alone while resisting arrest. Take no chances as he is very fast on the draw. When last seen, wore buckskin vest, tan pants, high-heeled boots and floppy hat. Deadly accurate shot. Antagonistic toward all police.'"

"Gee . . ." whispered Lippy. "He got into it, he did. I never thought—"

"Never mind thinking," thundered Gilman. "I'll do all the thinking there is to be done in this town. You know this gent?"

"Well . . . ah . . . that is . . . I . . . I met him once in a bar," said Lippy. "Yep, that was it. In a bar. I was standing there and somebody looked over and said, 'There's that Howdy Johnson.' And I said, 'Oh, is that Howdy Johnson?' And he said—"

"Well, just you let that gent show his face in here," threatened Gilman.

"Oh, I won't let him if I . . . I mean, I bet he is sure a long ways from here. I bet he's in California or maybe Oregon or maybe Canada or . . ."

A wagon creaked dismally in the street. A horse plodded to a stop. A cheerful, loud voice bawled, "Hello there, Lippy! You son of a gun, I ain't laid eyes on you for eight months and I shore—"

Lippy had turned by this time. His face was lard color. He beheld Howdy Johnson dismounted and striding forward with an outstretched hand.

Lippy achieved the ultimate in quick thinking. He shouted ten times louder than a steam whistle. He yelled, "If it ain't Bill! How the hell are you, Bill? Where you been, Bill?" all the time heading out and away from the Gila Monster's den.

Howdy looked puzzled. Howdy said, "Bill? What the dickens—"

"Yes sir, Bill," shrieked Lippy, cracking a vocal cord to drown Howdy out. "I sure am glad to see you, so help me. Where you been? How was Denver, Bill?"

All the time, Lippy was shoving the astounded Howdy far out of earshot. When he got him around the end of the Crystal Palace Saloon, Lippy leaned weakly against the side of the shack and mopped at his smudgy forehead with a quivering bandana.

"D-D-Don't do that again," pleaded Lippy. "Don't *ever* do that again. Look here, Howdy. You got your hoss right here. You fork him and light out quick, you hear me?"

"What's the trouble?" said Howdy, looking from Poison to Lippy.

"He was just inside that door," gasped Lippy. "And he'd just finished reading a reward poster that said you was wanted dead or alive in Chicago. And he said if you ever showed your nose in this town he'd kill you on sight. That's what's the matter."

"Oh, you mean the Gila Monster?" said Howdy.

"Sure. Who the hell do you think I meant? Saint Peter?"

"You boys sure seem upset," said Howdy.

"Upset!" cried Lippy. "Upset ain't no word for it. We're all suffering from nervous breakdowns, that's what. I'm gettin' so I can't even lift a drink to my mug without spillin' at least half of it."

"But he hadn't ought to bother you," said Howdy. "A general store is a plenty peaceful business even in Powderville."

"That's what you think," yelped Lippy. "That's what you think. I sell shootin' irons, don't I? Well, for every gun I sell I have to give Gilman twenty percent. For every cartridge I have to give him half price. For every pound of beans I sell I have to hand him ten cents. For every ham . . ." Lippy broke down. He could not bear the recounting of his woes. Finally he whispered, "They're gone, Howdy. Them good old days are gone. Powderville is quiet as a church. No scrappin', no arguin', no smokin' on Sunday . . ."

"Why didn't you move like Poison?"

"I tried," sobbed Lippy. "I tried to move, but it ain't like Poison. I run the only general store in the town and if I moved, he'd shoot me and run the place himself. I tried to get away

last month, but he trailed me and brought me back and said
he'd kill me if I tried it again. I got to stay open. I can't raise
my prices, but I got to pay his taxes. But you get out of here,
Howdy, and you get out quick before he recognizes you. I hate
to see an old pal slaughtered in cold blood, Howdy. I couldn't
stand it."

Howdy bridled. He brought one hairy fist smacking into
his palm. He snorted. He said, "You ain't got any civic pride
at all. Why don't you lay for this Gila Monster and some
night get him with a scatter-gun?"

"Jake did that," moaned Lippy, "and Gilman shot first.
Barney did that, and we buried him. Listen, Howdy. Just
stand there and listen. . . . There, did you hear anything?"

"Not a thing," said Howdy.

"There! Not a thing. Here it is five-thirty, just the time
things used to warm up, and what do you hear? Nothing. It's
like livin' in a grave, that's what. Yesterday I rode five miles
out of town and shot off two boxes of Henrys. Just to hear
them, you understand. But it made me feel so bad, I had to
quit. The town's gone to hell for keeps, Howdy."

"Ain't I one of the founders?" cried the indignant Howdy.
"Didn't you and me and Poison here start this place? Didn't
we agree I was to be the marshal from then on? Didn't I get
the post office in here and run it? Didn't I start the teamsters
bringing their loads through here? Didn't I make this the
finest trail-herd stop in the state? And you think I'll desert
the place? You think I'll stand here and let a rotten-bellied,
four-flushing, three-for-a-cent, slime-whiskered, two-gun
hog ride all over Powderville? No! I came back here—"

"But there's a poster in his office that says you're wanted," protested Lippy. "It says you killed three cops in Chicago. He read it."

"Well, who cares about three cops?" cried Howdy. "That's Chicago's lookout, that is. And if this sawed-down, black-livered—"

"But it says there's a reward," said Lippy.

"How much?"

"Fifteen hundred dollars. He'll do anything for that much money. It says to ship your body back and collect."

"Well, there's the hole in that. Everybody knows you couldn't ship a guy from here to Chicago and still recognize who he was. You *know* that. Here it is summer—"

"Please," begged Lippy. "You get out of town quick before we have to plant you."

"Nope," said Howdy. "I'll see Powderville through. I'll rid this fair city of the foul clutches of this steer-faced octopus. Gentlemen, before I see this man, before we measure his length in dirt, what say we adjourn for a drink?"

"All right," said Lippy in a shaken voice. "We still got fifteen minutes before the bars close."

Everybody was glad to see Howdy Johnson back, but not a single man failed to beg Howdy to leave Powderville. Howdy, they said, had never been known as a quick-draw, flashy gunfighter, and killing three cops in Chicago certainly could not be considered more than casual practice. Any man in the town of Powderville could have done that. Even Fanner Jones, they said, had bagged himself more than that in one day, and Fanner Jones was called Fanner because he couldn't fan.

No sir, said public opinion, Howdy was a damned fool to come back at all, especially when he had a reward on him. Howdy was just another bait for the Gila Monster to gobble up. It was a shame, everybody agreed, for Howdy to swell Gilman's purse by fifteen hundred dollars. It almost canceled out Howdy's civic pride.

At six the bar closed as per the directions of an erratically printed sign bearing Gilman's name, which was posted on a two-by-four just inside the door.

The men in the Crystal Palace, some twenty of them, nervously eyed Howdy and kept away from in back of him, just in case Gilman should glance in at the door. The more morbid citizens wandered in from the street and took seats along the wall.

Howdy had been talking with loud assurance, occasionally patting his holster, eternally pounding his hairy fist on the sticky table top. At six sharp, according to Lippy's watch, Howdy stood up. Everybody thought he looked a little nervous, though it was rather dim and it was hard to tell.

"If you'll pardon me, gents," said Howdy, "I think I'll take a stroll around. I ain't seen this fair city for eight whole months, and I craves to satisfy my artistic appetite."

Elbows nudged ribs. Men looked wise. Howdy turned and walked slowly out of the back door.

In a relieved way, Lippy said, "I was hoping he'd light out. I didn't want to see him murdered."

"Me neither," said Poison, "but I wish he hadn't convinced me about coming back. Now I got all that drive to make over again. Here I wasted three weeks and nothing at all to show for it. But still, I'm happy he didn't stay."

Fanner Jones sneered, "He talked pretty big for a while there, didn't he?"

A stranger at the bar chuckled about it and said, "This Gila Monster must be pretty bad if a man lights out before he even sees him."

"You said it, mister," said Lippy. "He's the toughest—"

"Shhhhh," hissed Poison.

Gilman could be heard outside. Boards cracked and splintered from his weight on the walk. The steps into the saloon groaned. The doors slammed inward and jarred loose their slats and there stood the Gila Monster, eyebrows close together and hovering like thunderheads.

"Is a gent named Howdy Johnson in here?" snarled Gilman.

"Er . . . aw . . . uh . . . he just left," croaked the barkeep.

"Just left, did he? Well, you tell him, if you see him, that I want a talk with him. I want to convince him that this Powderville is the most peaceful, law-abiding town in the state. You tell him I invite him over any time he wants. There ain't no posted gunslinger going to sneak into Powderville while *I* know it."

"Of course not," said Lippy.

"What?"

"I said . . . I said, 'Of course not!'"

"Your tone wasn't very civil," snapped Gilman, fingering

his gun hopefully. "You— Say, you're Poison Peters! You there. What's the idea of trying to run out on Powderville, huh? Well, you showed sense. You come back."

"I . . . I'm leaving pretty quick," said Poison.

"That's what *you* think," roared Gilman. "You're going to open up the Bucket-o'-Blood, so help me. Come on, come on. Pay up. To open a saloon in Powderville costs just one hundred dollars."

"But I . . . I had a saloon open here and . . ."

"You callin' me a liar?"

"No, no, no. No, of course not! A hundred dollars, you said? There."

"That's better," said Gilman, grinning ghoulishly and pocketing the cash. "Now you can open up any time you like. You can't sell liquor here after six. But still, you opened up today, so I'll have to have the additional fifty dollars that's charged all law-abiding saloonkeepers today."

"B-B-But I haven't—"

Gilman swooped and sank pitchfork fingers into Poison's shoulder. Poison's chair threw him and Poison lit in the sandbox. Gilman's eyes were alight with glee.

Poison quickly fished out fifty dollars and paid.

"That's better," chuckled Gilman. "That's better. We got to have taxes for roads and schools and things."

The stranger at the bar smiled and said, "I didn't see any schools, nor roads either for that matter."

Gilman turned carefully. He slouched forward and looked down upon the crown of the stranger's hat.

"Who the hell are you?" said Gilman pleasantly.

"I'm riding advance of the Slash Bar trail herd," said the stranger.

"Now that's fine, Mr. Trail Boss," said Gilman with an affable snarl. "I got a nice town here and you'll stop, of course."

"I don't think so," said the stranger. "I see you're still alive and so I think we'll head for Dead Horse Hole to water."

"No water there, brother. At least, what is there got poisoned last month by a couple wolfers, so I hear. You'll stop in Powderville and like it."

That settled, Gilman took a drink, grinned like a crocodile and said to the room in general, "If you see this Howdy Johnson, tell him he's plumb careless with his horseflesh and his saddlebags. You tell him, if he wants them, to come and see me about it. You tell him he ain't got a thing to be scared of as everybody knows how humane I am. You tell him I don't like to see men suffer none and so I always blow their hearts through their spines the first shot to prevent pain. That's my message, gents. The evil elements of society ain't got a chance in Powderville and they knows it from the Pecos to Hudson Bay."

Steps groaned, the sidewalk creaked, Gilman was gone.

The saloon was held in the grip of chilly silence. The only sound in Powderville came from the faraway blacksmith shop, and the hammer and anvil sound reminded everybody of a coffin maker's trade.

Soon incautious Howdy would be ferreted out. Soon there would be a shot. Powderville would file out to view the last remains of Johnson.

Poor fellow.

Night progressed. A prairie wind came up and whined dismally around the scabby buildings as though saddened by the contamination. Oil lamps flickered. The road was a patchwork quilt of yellow and black.

And still no shot.

And still no Howdy.

Hours were nerve-stretching racks. Men huddled in silent, tight groups in the dingy shacks, still listening, unwilling to walk outside lest any one of them be mistaken for the Gila Monster's quarry.

And still no shot.

At midnight Lippy whispered to Poison, "He must have left the country."

"On foot?" said Poison.

"He might of stole a hoss," said Lippy.

"I guess you're right, Lippy. Blood and bone can stand just so much."

The listless barkeep said, "I knew it was too good to be true. Howdy knowed he wasn't good enough. Lucky he got away in time, I says. No use for this here Gila Monster to carve *all* the butt from his irons."

The lingering stranger grinned. "He talked big while he lasted. But looks to me like it'd take more'n air to blow down this here Gilman. You couldn't hire my boys to tangle with him. Not for a million million, you couldn't. Still, it ain't tasteful for a man to brag like that."

"I guess it ain't," said Fanner Jones. "I always knowed that Howdy was a lot of wind."

Lippy stood up. "No sense waitin' any longer. The light's gone out in Gilman's office. I'm for beddin' down."

The citizens of Powderville agreed with him, as it was long after midnight. Besides, you couldn't see to dig until morning. And Howdy Johnson, for all his talk, had undoubtedly hit trail.

Morning came and found Powderville still viced in silence. The gray tombstone buildings stood mute and forlorn upon the prairie, holding forth no promise. Powderville had died. Only the ghosts of memory prowled, and even they were hushed lest they displease Gilman.

That day found Gilman in high spirits. He spent a great deal of his time laughing—or rather, emitting a nasty buzz-saw sound which passed for laughter.

He told the Powderville citizens one and all that a thorough search of the place had not revealed a trace of the missing man. He told Powderville that the mere mention of the Gilman name was enough to make criminals shudder from Maine to California. He said he had kept his promise. Six months before, he had entered the town. He had stated that Powderville needed taming. This flight of a gunman would stand forever as the lasting and final proof to the law-abiding reputation of Powderville.

And though the town mourned in private, it was quick to agree that Powderville was obviously and forever tamed.

Toward evening the Slash Bar herd could be seen in the distance. The brown dust cloud stopped a good mile from the town and settled there. Soon the chuck wagon could be seen spewing black smoke, and riders came in and turned their horses into the remuda.

In vain Powderville waited for business, but by five-thirty it was quite apparent that none of the Slash Bar crowd wanted anything to do with a thoroughly tamed cow town run by such a thoroughly untamed, self-elected marshal. The Slash Bar would use the water hole out there, would push through to the railroad in the north, without enriching Powderville by so much as a plugged *peso*. As Powderville had been built and run by and for trail herds, this was a signal of ultimate and speedy ruin.

Long-faced merchants moped in their doors. The worthy citizens whittled disconsolately on steps. The Gila Monster lounged in his office, not in the least perturbed.

At five-thirty-five, the reopened Bucket-o'-Blood received a horrible shock. The gentlemen gathered there, already in the lowest depths of melancholy, were shaken.

Howdy Johnson stepped into the back door.

He walked to a table.

He sat down.

He ordered a drink.

Poison tried to pour it for him, but the amber fluid splashed on the bar from the wobbling bottle, unable to hit the shaking glass.

Petrified, the other customers sat right where they were and stared.

"Howdy, Poison. Looks like the Slash Bar crowd is staying on its bed-ground."

Poison swallowed hard. It was gruesome, the way Howdy sat there talking about such small matters. In a matter of minutes Howdy would be stretched on dark-stained boards and the silence of the town would be cut by scraping shovels.

Poor fellow.

"We . . . we thought you'd left," said Lippy.

"Me?" said Howdy. "ME? Leave Powderville? I should say not. I should say *not*."

"But Gilman said—" moaned Poison.

"Pish for what Gilman said," replied Howdy in an airy way. "Gentlemen, I stated last night that I was going to save Powderville from the talons of this stinking buzzard. That I aims to do. Powderville, gentlemen, will live again. In the rosy future, I foresee a rough, tough, wild and hilarious existence."

"P-P-Please," said Poison. "Beat it, Howdy, I couldn't stand to see you shot. Look here, Gilman will be in at six to make sure I've closed the bar and to collect the take. He'll see you and kill you. Honest he will, Howdy. I got a look at that reward poster and it sure has put him hot on your trail. It says you're bad. It's a direct challenge to Gilman's gunning ability. If he don't shoot you, he'll lose prestige, so you can see for yourself that there ain't no way for you to talk yourself out of it. At six—"

"At six," beamed Howdy, "you go right on dispensing drinks."

"WHAT?"

"You heard me," said Howdy. "Gentlemen, the curfew will not ring tonight."

"Oh, yes, it will," said Lippy. "Gilman will see to that."

Howdy took out a big silver watch and laid it face up before him. Behind it he ranged a rank of full glasses. He marked the time.

Five minutes passed, making it twenty minutes to six.

Howdy took a drink.

Another five minutes crept by.

Howdy took another drink.

"Three drinks to go," Howdy informed them. "By the way, it's sure sinful the way the evil sleep. I heard a lot said about the snoring of the just, but there ain't nothing in it at all. . . ."

Five long minutes.

Another drink.

The *tic-tic-tickety-tic* of Howdy's watch raced merrily along. Powderville drifted slowly in, pale of face and jittery, watching the man soon to be a corpse.

"You got five dollars?" said Lippy.

"Sure, I got five dollars," said Howdy.

"Then we won't have to take up a fund," mourned Lippy.

Five minutes.

A drink.

Tic-tic-tickety-tic went that awful watch.

Citizens carefully left a wide path between Howdy and the door, and left the space from his back to the wall scrupulously vacant.

Howdy hummed a little song.

Six o'clock.

The last drink went down.

Howdy sat entrenched behind the watch and the empty glasses. He did not bother to listen or keep an eye on the door.

*Citizens carefully left a wide path between Howdy
and the door, and left the space from his back
to the wall scrupulously vacant.*

Poison nervously began to put away the bottles.

"No need of that," said Howdy. "That Slash Bar outfit will be in here before the night's out."

The crowd watched him closely as though he were a man of quite a different race, a sideshow freak. They only lacked the purple-gray gloves to be thirty pallbearers.

"He's late," whispered Lippy.

Tic-tic-tickety-tic.

Creak, creak, creak came Gilman's footsteps on the walk. The planks groaned, the porch sagged in terror, the swinging doors volleyed and there stood the Gila Monster.

There are men who will say that a silver-tip grizzly raised upright to the height of eight feet is a terrifying sight, but wiser men know that anyone making that declaration had never seen Gilman.

His boots reared out of the floor like two gigantic redwood stumps. His legs went upward like telegraph poles. His body hulked skyward like Pike's Peak. His head filled a hat big enough to make half a dozen tents. And his arms hung down like two boa constrictors ready for the kill.

His lantern-globe eyes had caught the full blow of Howdy's presence. He looked carefully, leaning forward, looked away and stabbed his awful glance again.

A smile opened a gash like the Grand Canyon on the Gila Monster's face. His arms began to swing and he wet his lips with a tongue as black and long as a muleskinner's whip.

A sound started way down in the caverns of his belly, rumbled upward, shaking the whole room, and emerged so loud a laugh of glee that it cracked the mirror over the bar.

Leather groaned as his holsters were relieved of the weights of his twin cannon. He spun the guns by the trigger guards.

"You're getting an even break!" thundered Gilman, centering his sights on Howdy's heart. "You draw!"

Howdy sat stiffly. It was difficult for him to move.

He snapped out his Colt.

Twin blasts streaked away from the Gila Monster's muzzles.

Howdy jerked backward and sagged over his table in front.

Gilman chuckled and the room quivered. He blew the smoke from the muzzle and cylinder, lazy and lethal.

Everybody stared at poor Howdy. Two holes were in his vest, just over his heart. His gun lay slackly in his stiff hand upon the table top.

As though in his death agony, Howdy's fist clenched spasmodically.

A look of stony surprise crept down like a mask over the Gila Monster's face.

Gilman staggered.

A third eye was blue and blind in his forehead.

Knees buckling, gun falling, shoulders slouching, Gilman dropped. He toppled slowly like a felled tree at first. Then faster.

At full length he hit. The floor crunched beneath his weight. His legs doubled and shot out straight again, making his spurs jangle.

His hands slowly relaxed.

"They're dead," whispered Lippy.

The citizens crept fearfully forward and stooped over the collapsed giant. Boots and hands rolled him over. His arms fell limply outward, his black mouth was agape, his eyes were fixed in a steely stare.

"Poor Howdy," choked Poison. "Poor Howdy. He give up his life to rid us of disaster. But his noble sacrifice shall never be forgotten. We shall build a monument to his civic pride that his fame shall forever endure. Gentlemen, let us drink to the unselfish heroism of Howdy..."

"Make mine rye," said Howdy, pocketing his silver watch. Not a man moved.

"I said 'rye,'" repeated Howdy, grinning.

They gave him rye. They gave him quarts and barrels of rye. They set before him all the rye in Powderville and helped him drink it down.

They plied him with questions, they ladened him with praise. But Howdy just sat and drank and grinned.

The Slash Bar crew heard the news and rode hilariously in. Guns banged in the streets. Three mirrors were splintered in the first hour. Before nine o'clock five fights had started. By ten, a man had to shout to be heard more than two feet.

In the midst of happy bedlam sat Howdy. He beamed with fatherly pride. He was fondly observing the feet of his workmanlike job which protruded from under the pool table.

Poison, weary of dispensing, at last found a moment to talk.

"Howdy, anything you want is yours. Anything! Whatever you'd like to have us gents do for you, just speak up. We won't ask you how you done it; we won't ask nothing but the privilege of honoring your presence amongst us. What'll you have, Howdy?"

"If it won't be no bother," said Howdy, peering over a glass rim and digging into his shirt, "there's a couple bills I can't square on account of not having no money."

Poison took them and read them.

THE RINGTAIL PRINTING SHOP

Printing 50 reward posters for
H. Johnson . . . . . $5 bucks

"Then," gasped Poison, "that Chicago shooting was just a come-on! But—"

The other bill said:

POWDERVILLE BLACKSMITHY

Fine Shoeing and Iron Work
Howdy Johnson . . . . . $25.00 bucks
For tailoring one ¼ in. sheet-iron shirt as per specification.
J. Olsen, prop.

Story Preview

Story Preview

NOW that you've just ventured through some of the captivating tales in the Stories from the Golden Age collection by L. Ron Hubbard, turn the page and enjoy a preview of *Cattle King for a Day*. Join Chinook Shannon as he seeks the real identity of the man who killed his grandfather and is now after his ranch—with forgery, sabotage and murder riding by his side.

Cattle King for a Day

A CROSS the street the swinging doors of the Diamond Palace jumped outward. Two hard-looking riders strode down the steps and started to cross the street.

Chinook did not have to be told that these two were part of Kendall's outfit. Somehow, all of Kendall's men were of a similar stamp.

Chinook flipped Kendall's hog leg out and into a pile of straw. The oldster scurried into the dimness, still covering Kendall.

"Come on," said the bowlegged one to Chinook. "Don't stand there gawping. We've got to get the hell out of here before them two arrive."

Led hurriedly out through the rear of the building, Chinook had no time to speculate upon his savior's identity and the oldster seemed to take it as a matter of course that Chinook knew.

They skirted the back of the livery stable, walking over piles of rubbish and, at the bowlegged one's request, entered another smaller shack which had barred windows.

A man with a big nose and flabby jowls looked up from a newspaper, over his upraised boot toes and at the two callers. A large star was prominent upon his chest.

"Hello, Deke," said the sheriff. "Who's your friend?"

"He's Chinook Shannon. Can't you tell it? You always was

blind in one eye. You got to give him a hand. Kendall was just trying to knock him off over in the barn."

"My, my," said the sheriff, rubbing his nose and looking apprehensively at the door. "Er . . . aw . . . do you suppose they know he came in here, Deke?"

"No, they think maybe he rode away. Shannon, in spite of that jackrabbit expression on his face, this is Sheriff Taggart. Your grandpappy put him in office."

Chinook shook Taggart's flabby, wet hand.

"In case your grandpappy never mentioned me to you, I'm Deacon Murphy, his foreman."

"Pleased to meet you," said Chinook. "Now that we're all properly introduced, let me inquire about this Kendall. How come he's running Bull Butte?"

"Took it over this spring," said Deke. "The son of a jackass took over a mine up Pan Creek, poisoned all our stock with cyanide and raised hell in general. Damn him, he didn't fight square. He murdered your grandpappy and then went over the rest of us like a prairie fire. The boys scattered to hell and gone but I've hung around Bull Butte for two months waiting for you to come. And now that you're here, you've only got the place for a day and we can't do anything in that length of time."

"How about the courts?" said Chinook.

"Er . . . aw . . . ahumph," said Taggart. "When the circuit judge came . . . er . . . Deke Murphy was the only witness that could be got—"

"Because you was scared to testify," snapped Deke, rubbing emphatically at his gray whiskers. "But what you going to do, son?"

"Murphy," said Shannon, "the least I can do is nail the man that shot my grandfather."

"Kendall," said Deke.

"And I can at least make a try to save the Slash S."

"Borden's got his bug eye on it," said Deke.

"I know. I've talked to him. Murphy, all my life I've wanted to be what they call a cattle king. I've drifted around and I've never really amounted to much. Well, I'm one now, if only for twenty-four hours. Sheriff, if I shoot it out with this crowd, where do I stand with you?"

"Well . . . aw . . . er . . . ahumph . . . aw . . . that is, if you were to get all of them, Shannon, *all of them,* I think you would find me quite agreeable. But I . . . er . . . aw . . . cannot countenance any slaughter which would . . . aw . . . fail to clean out them *all.* You are, after all, Shannon, but one man and they are twenty-one. I am afraid . . ."

"You don't have to tell him how scared you are," snapped Deke. "If we get them all, is it to be an even break in the eyes of the law?"

"An uneven break," said Taggart, "if you should ask me. I am afraid, Deke, that this young man is committing suicide—"

"That's my lookout," said Chinook. "First, Murphy, we'd better look over the Slash S and that mine. Sheriff, you'll please give us a hand in getting our horses?"

"Not me," said Taggart, definitely.

"Then you cover me, Murphy," said Chinook. "Daylight's burning."

To find out more about *Cattle King for a Day* and how you can obtain your copy, go to www.goldenagestories.com.

Glossary

Glossary

STORIES FROM THE GOLDEN AGE *reflect the words and expressions used in the 1930s and 1940s, adding unique flavor and authenticity to the tales. While a character's speech may often reflect regional origins, it also can convey attitudes common in the day. So that readers can better grasp such cultural and historical terms, uncommon words or expressions of the era, the following glossary has been provided.*

---

angoras: chaps (leather leggings the cowboy wears to protect his legs) made of goat hide with the hair left on.

barker: a gun.

batwings: long chaps (leather leggings the cowboy wears to protect his legs) with big flaps of leather. They usually fasten with rings and snaps.

beller: bellow; to emit a hollow, loud animal cry.

blamed: confounded.

blow "charge": to sound a bugle call that signals cavalry to go into battle.

bunghole: the hole in a liquid-tight barrel. The hole is capped with a large corklike object called a *bung*.

bung starter: a wooden mallet used for tapping on the bung (cork or stopper) to loosen it from a barrel.

calaboose: a jail.

carbines: short light rifles, originally used by soldiers on horses.

cayuse: used by the northern cowboy in referring to any horse. At first the term was used for the Western horse to set it apart from a horse brought overland from the East. Later the name was applied as a term of contempt to any scrubby, undersized horse. Named after the Cayuse Indian tribe.

Chi: Chicago.

chuck: food.

chuck wagon: a mess wagon of the cow country. It is usually made by fitting, at the back end of an ordinary farm wagon, a large box that contains shelves and has a hinged lid fitted with legs that serves as a table when lowered. The chuck wagon is a cowboy's home on the range, where he keeps his bedroll and dry clothes, gets his food and has a warm fire.

Colt: a single-action, six-shot cylinder revolver, most commonly available in .45- or .44-caliber versions. It was first manufactured in 1873 for the Army by the Colt Firearms Company, the armory founded by American inventor Samuel Colt (1814–1862) who revolutionized the firearms industry with the invention of the revolver. The Colt, also known as the Peacemaker, was also made available to civilians. As a reliable, inexpensive and popular handgun among cowboys, it became known as the "cowboy's gun" and a symbol of the Old West.

concha: a disk, traditionally of hammered silver and resembling a shell or flower, used as a decoration piece on belts, harnesses, etc.

coup stick: a stick with which some North American Indian warriors sought to touch their enemies in battle as a sign of courage.

cow town: a town at the end of the trail from which cattle were shipped; later applied to towns in the cattle country that depended upon the cowman and his trade for their existence.

crust: nerve.

cyanide: an extremely poisonous compound. It is used in mining as a method of extracting gold and other metals from raw ore. Cyanide is applied to the ore, where it bonds with microscopic flecks of gold that are then recovered from the cyanide solution.

dast: dare.

'dobe: short for adobe; a building constructed with sun-dried bricks made from clay.

dry washes: dry stream beds, as at the bottom of a canyon.

end man: a man at each end of the line of performers in a minstrel show who engages in comic banter with the master of ceremonies. A minstrel show is a comic variety show presenting jokes, songs, dances and skits, usually by white actors in blackface.

fan: to fire a series of shots (from a single-action revolver) by holding the trigger back and successively striking the hammer to the rear with the free hand.

faro: a gambling game played with cards and popular in the American West of the nineteenth century. In faro, the players bet on the order in which the cards will be turned over by the dealer. The cards were kept in a dealing box to keep track of the play.

fork: mount (a horse).

foundered: gone lame.

four-flushing: fake, phony or fraudulent; characteristic of someone who bluffs or otherwise can't back up his bragging.

foxed: trimmed.

G-men: government men; agents of the Federal Bureau of Investigation.

gold-chased revolvers: gold-engraved metal, as ornamentation on a gun.

hair pants: chaps (leather leggings the cowboy wears to protect his legs) made with hair-covered hide.

Hannibal: (247–183 BC) Carthaginian general (the ancient city of Carthage was on the coast of North Africa) whose march on Rome from Spain across the Alps remains one of the greatest feats in military history.

hard-boiled shirt: clean shirt; also called a "boiled-collar shirt" as the removable collar was often boiled clean, separately, to allow for an extra day or two's wear. The collars were often stiff and uncomfortable because they were heavily starched.

Henry: the first rifle to use a cartridge with a metallic casing rather than the undependable, self-contained powder, ball and primer of previous rifles. It was named after B. Tyler Henry, who designed the rifle and the cartridge.

Henrys: cartridges designed by B. Tyler Henry for use in the Henry rifle. The metallic cartridge case, made of copper or brass, had the primer inside a folded rim and contained 25 grains of gunpowder.

hog leg: another name for the popular Colt revolver also known as the Peacemaker.

hogshead: a large barrel or cask with a capacity ranging from 63 to 140 gallons.

hogtied: tied up with all four hands and feet together.

hombres: men, especially in the Southwest. Sometimes it implies rough fellows, toughs; often it means real men.

hone: to yearn; long.

hoss: horse.

howitzers: cannons that have comparatively short barrels, used especially for firing shells at a high angle of elevation for a short range, as for reaching a target behind cover or in a trench.

Hudson Bay: a large inland sea in the northeast of Canada. On the east it is connected with the Atlantic Ocean and on the north with the Arctic Ocean.

iron: a handgun, especially a revolver.

Laredo: a city of southern Texas on the Rio Grande.

lariat: a long noosed rope used for catching horses, cattle, etc.; lasso.

light out: to leave quickly; depart hurriedly.

lights: to land; come to rest.

lobo: wolf; one who is regarded as predatory, greedy and fierce.

lobo wolf: gray wolf.

longhorn: a mean and temperamental person, from the name given the early cattle of Texas because of the enormous spread of their horns that served for attack and defense. Longhorns were not only mean, but the slightest provocation, especially with a bull, would turn them into an aggressive and dangerous enemy. Used figuratively here.

lucifer: a match.

macheer saddle: a saddle covered with a piece of heavy leather called a *mochila*. The *mochila*, Americanized by the cowhand to *macheer*, was split at both ends to fit around the horn and cantle and covered the whole saddle.

man alive: used as an intensive or exclamation.

minstrel show: a comic variety show presenting jokes, songs, dances and skits, usually by white actors in blackface.

monte: a card game in which two cards are chosen from four laid out face up, and a player bets that one of the two cards will be matched in suit by the dealer before the other one.

muleskinner: someone who drives mules.

Nevadas: Sierra Nevada mountain range of eastern California, extending between the Sacramento and San Joaquin valleys and the Nevada border.

opines: thinks; supposes.

Peacemaker: nickname for the single-action (that is, cocked by hand for each shot), six-shot Army model revolver first produced in 1873 by the Colt Firearms Company, the armory founded by Samuel Colt (1814–1862). The handgun of the Old West, it became the instrument of both lawmaker and lawbreaker during the last twenty-five years of the nineteenth century. It soon earned various names, such as "hog leg," "Equalizer," and "Judge Colt and his jury of six."

Pecos: a city in western Texas and near the southern border of New Mexico.

pemmican: a traditional native North American food made with strips of lean dried meat pounded into a paste, mixed with melted fat and dried berries or fruits and pressed into small cakes.

Pike's Peak: a mountain, 14,110 feet high, in the Rocky Mountains in central Colorado.

plugged *peso:* a worthless coin.

port: the position of a rifle or other weapon when it is held with both hands in a slanting direction across the front of the body, with the barrel near the left shoulder.

postin': posting; rising and sinking in the saddle, in accordance with the motion of the horse, especially in trotting while riding using an English saddle.

prop: proprietor.

puncher: a hired hand who tends cattle and performs other duties on horseback.

quirt: a riding whip with a short handle and a braided leather lash.

remuda: a group of saddle horses from which ranch hands pick mounts for the day.

riata: a long noosed rope used to catch animals.

rimfire saddle: a saddle with one cinch that is placed far to the front; also called a *Spanish rig* or *rimmy.*

romals: extensions to the reins that function as riding whips.

rowels: the small spiked revolving wheels on the ends of spurs, which are attached to the heels of a rider's boots and used to nudge a horse into going faster.

running irons: branding irons that are not bent into the shape of the mark, but rather require the user to write the desired brand.

saddle boot: a close-fitting covering or case for a gun or other weapon that straps to a saddle.

Saint Peter: the most prominent of the twelve disciples of Jesus Christ.

sandbox: a primitive sort of spittoon, consisting of a wooden box filled with sand.

scabby: covered with *scabs,* short, flat pieces of wood used for binding two pieces of timber that are butted together, or for strengthening timber at weak spots.

scatter-gun: a cowboy's name for a shotgun.

Scheherazade: the female narrator of *The Arabian Nights,* who during one thousand and one adventurous nights saved her life by entertaining her husband, the king, with stories.

scrappin': scrapping; disagreeing; fighting.

Sharps: any of several models of firearms devised by Christian Sharps and produced by the Sharps Rifle Company until 1881. The most popular Sharps were "Old Reliable," the cavalry carbine, and the heavy-caliber, single-shot buffalo-hunting rifle. Because of its low muzzle velocity, this gun was said to "fire today, kill tomorrow."

shootin' irons: handguns.

shorthorn: a tenderfoot; a newcomer or a person not used to rough living and hardships.

Sierras: Sierra Nevada mountain range of eastern California extending between the Sacramento and San Joaquin valleys and the Nevada border.

slick-ear: 1. a range animal lacking an earmark; an unbranded and unmarked animal. 2. "wet behind the ears"; someone who is inexperienced or naïve.

sougan: bedroll; a blanket or quilt with a protective canvas tarp for use on a bunk or on the range.

sowbelly: salt pork; pork cured in salt, especially fatty pork from the back, side or belly of a hog.

Stetson: as the most popular broad-brimmed hat in the West, it became the generic name for *hat*. John B. Stetson was a master hat maker and founder of the company that has been making Stetsons since 1865. Not only can the Stetson stand up to a terrific amount of beating, the cowboy's hat has more different uses than any other garment he wears. It keeps the sun out of the eyes and off the neck; it serves as an umbrella; it makes a great fan, which sometimes is needed when building a fire or shunting cattle about; the brim serves as a cup to water oneself, or as a bucket to water the horse or put out the fire.

stint: restrain; restrict.

string: a group of animals, especially saddle horses, owned or used by one person.

tapaderos: heavy leather around the front of stirrups to protect the rider's foot.

taps: a bugle call or drum signal sounded at military funerals and memorial services.

teamsters: individuals who drive a team of horses, especially in hauling freight.

trail herd: a herd of cattle driven along a trail, especially from their home range to market.

Waterloo, had his: variation of "meet your Waterloo," meaning that one who has previously been successful has been defeated by someone who is too strong for one. It comes from the "Battle of Waterloo," fought in 1815, which was Napoleon's last battle. This defeat put a final end to his rule.

wet gunnysacking: a branding technique used by rustlers. Branding is done through a wet gunnysack, making a temporary brand that looks permanent.

whittled: carved something out of wood, usually something small enough to hold in the hand, by cutting away small pieces.

wolfer: a man hired by a rancher to trap and hunt wolves on his range.

wrangler: a cowboy who takes care of the saddle horses.

L. Ron Hubbard
in the Golden Age
of Pulp Fiction

In writing an adventure story
a writer has to know that he is adventuring
for a lot of people who cannot.
The writer has to take them here and there
about the globe and show them
excitement and love and realism.
As long as that writer is living the part of an
adventurer when he is hammering
the keys, he is succeeding with his story.

Adventuring is a state of mind.
If you adventure through life, you have a
good chance to be a success on paper.

Adventure doesn't mean globe-trotting,
exactly, and it doesn't mean great deeds.
Adventuring is like art.
You have to live it to make it real.

— *L. RON HUBBARD*

L. Ron Hubbard
and American
Pulp Fiction

B ORN March 13, 1911, L. Ron Hubbard lived a life at least as expansive as the stories with which he enthralled a hundred million readers through a fifty-year career.

Originally hailing from Tilden, Nebraska, he spent his formative years in a classically rugged Montana, replete with the cowpunchers, lawmen and desperadoes who would later people his Wild West adventures. And lest anyone imagine those adventures were drawn from vicarious experience, he was not only breaking broncs at a tender age, he was also among the few whites ever admitted into Blackfoot society as a bona fide blood brother. While if only to round out an otherwise rough and tumble youth, his mother was that rarity of her time—a thoroughly educated woman—who introduced her son to the classics of Occidental literature even before his seventh birthday.

But as any dedicated L. Ron Hubbard reader will attest, his world extended far beyond Montana. In point of fact, and as the son of a United States naval officer, by the age of eighteen he had traveled over a quarter of a million miles. Included therein were three Pacific crossings to a then still mysterious Asia, where he ran with the likes of Her British Majesty's agent-in-place

L. Ron Hubbard, left, at Congressional Airport, Washington, DC, 1931, with members of George Washington University flying club.

for North China, and the last in the line of Royal Magicians from the court of Kublai Khan. For the record, L. Ron Hubbard was also among the first Westerners to gain admittance to forbidden Tibetan monasteries below Manchuria, and his photographs of China's Great Wall long graced American geography texts.

Upon his return to the United States and a hasty completion of his interrupted high school education, the young Ron Hubbard entered George Washington University. There, as fans of his aerial adventures may have heard, he earned his wings as a pioneering barnstormer at the dawn of American aviation. He also earned a place in free-flight record books for the longest sustained flight above Chicago. Moreover, as a roving reporter for *Sportsman Pilot* (featuring his first professionally penned articles), he further helped inspire a generation of pilots who would take America to world airpower.

Immediately beyond his sophomore year, Ron embarked on the first of his famed ethnological expeditions, initially to then untrammeled Caribbean shores (descriptions of which would later fill a whole series of West Indies mystery-thrillers). That the Puerto Rican interior would also figure into the future of Ron Hubbard stories was likewise no accident. For in addition to cultural studies of the island, a 1932–33

LRH expedition is rightly remembered as conducting the first complete mineralogical survey of a Puerto Rico under United States jurisdiction.

There was many another adventure along this vein: As a lifetime member of the famed Explorers Club, L. Ron Hubbard charted North Pacific waters with the first shipboard radio direction finder, and so pioneered a long-range navigation system universally employed until the late twentieth century. While not to put too fine an edge on it, he also held a rare Master Mariner's license to pilot any vessel, of any tonnage in any ocean.

Yet lest we stray too far afield, there is an LRH note at this juncture in his saga, and it reads in part:

"I started out writing for the pulps, writing the best I knew, writing for every mag on the stands, slanting as well as I could."

To which one might add: His earliest submissions date from the summer of 1934, and included tales drawn from true-to-life Asian adventures, with characters roughly modeled on British/American intelligence operatives he had known in Shanghai. His early Westerns were similarly peppered with details drawn from personal experience. Although therein lay a first hard lesson from the often cruel world of the pulps. His first Westerns were soundly rejected as lacking the authenticity of a Max Brand yarn

Capt. L. Ron Hubbard in Ketchikan, Alaska, 1940, on his Alaskan Radio Experimental Expedition, the first of three voyages conducted under the Explorers Club flag.

(a particularly frustrating comment given L. Ron Hubbard's Westerns came straight from his Montana homeland, while Max Brand was a mediocre New York poet named Frederick Schiller Faust, who turned out implausible six-shooter tales from the terrace of an Italian villa).

Nevertheless, and needless to say, L. Ron Hubbard persevered and soon earned a reputation as among the most publishable names in pulp fiction, with a ninety percent placement rate of first-draft manuscripts. He was also among the most prolific, averaging between seventy and a hundred thousand words a month. Hence the rumors that L. Ron Hubbard had redesigned a typewriter for faster keyboard action and pounded out manuscripts on a continuous roll of butcher paper to save the precious seconds it took to insert a single sheet of paper into manual typewriters of the day.

That all L. Ron Hubbard stories did not run beneath said byline is yet another aspect of pulp fiction lore. That is, as publishers periodically rejected manuscripts from top-drawer authors if only to avoid paying top dollar, L. Ron Hubbard and company just as frequently replied with submissions under various pseudonyms. In Ron's case, the

A MAN OF MANY NAMES

Between 1934 and 1950, L. Ron Hubbard authored more than fifteen million words of fiction in more than two hundred classic publications. To supply his fans and editors with stories across an array of genres and pulp titles, he adopted fifteen pseudonyms in addition to his already renowned L. Ron Hubbard byline.

Winchester Remington Colt
Lt. Jonathan Daly
Capt. Charles Gordon
Capt. L. Ron Hubbard
Bernard Hubbel
Michael Keith
Rene Lafayette
Legionnaire 148
Legionnaire 14830
Ken Martin
Scott Morgan
Lt. Scott Morgan
Kurt von Rachen
Barry Randolph
Capt. Humbert Reynolds

list included: Rene Lafayette, Captain Charles Gordon, Lt. Scott Morgan and the notorious Kurt von Rachen—supposedly on the lam for a murder rap, while hammering out two-fisted prose in Argentina. The point: While L. Ron Hubbard as Ken Martin spun stories of Southeast Asian intrigue, LRH as Barry Randolph authored tales of

L. Ron Hubbard, circa 1930, at the outset of a literary career that would finally span half a century.

romance on the Western range—which, stretching between a dozen genres is how he came to stand among the two hundred elite authors providing close to a million tales through the glory days of American Pulp Fiction.

In evidence of exactly that, by 1936 L. Ron Hubbard was literally leading pulp fiction's elite as president of New York's American Fiction Guild. Members included a veritable pulp hall of fame: Lester "Doc Savage" Dent, Walter "The Shadow" Gibson, and the legendary Dashiell Hammett—to cite but a few.

Also in evidence of just where L. Ron Hubbard stood within his first two years on the American pulp circuit: By the spring of 1937, he was ensconced in Hollywood, adopting a Caribbean thriller for Columbia Pictures, remembered today as *The Secret of Treasure Island*. Comprising fifteen thirty-minute episodes, the L. Ron Hubbard screenplay led to the most profitable matinée serial in Hollywood history. In accord with Hollywood culture, he was thereafter continually called upon

The 1937 Secret of Treasure Island, *a fifteen-episode serial adapted for the screen by L. Ron Hubbard from his novel,* Murder at Pirate Castle.

to rewrite/doctor scripts—most famously for long-time friend and fellow adventurer Clark Gable.

In the interim—and herein lies another distinctive chapter of the L. Ron Hubbard story—he continually worked to open Pulp Kingdom gates to up-and-coming authors. Or, for that matter, anyone who wished to write. It was a fairly unconventional stance, as markets were already thin and competition razor sharp. But the fact remains, it was an L. Ron Hubbard hallmark that he vehemently lobbied on behalf of young authors—regularly supplying instructional articles to trade journals, guest-lecturing to short story classes at George Washington University and Harvard, and even founding his own creative writing competition. It was established in 1940, dubbed the Golden Pen, and guaranteed winners both New York representation and publication in *Argosy*.

But it was John W. Campbell Jr.'s *Astounding Science Fiction* that finally proved the most memorable LRH vehicle. While every fan of L. Ron Hubbard's galactic epics undoubtedly knows the story, it nonetheless bears repeating: By late 1938, the pulp publishing magnate of Street & Smith was determined to revamp *Astounding Science Fiction* for broader readership. In particular, senior editorial director F. Orlin Tremaine called for stories with a stronger *human element*. When acting editor John W. Campbell balked, preferring his spaceship-driven tales, Tremaine enlisted Hubbard. Hubbard, in turn, replied with the genre's first truly *character-driven* works, wherein heroes are pitted not against bug-eyed monsters but the mystery and majesty of deep space itself—and thus was launched the Golden Age of Science Fiction.

The names alone are enough to quicken the pulse of any science fiction aficionado, including LRH friend and protégé, Robert Heinlein, Isaac Asimov, A. E. van Vogt and Ray Bradbury. Moreover, when coupled with LRH stories of fantasy, we further come to what's rightly been described as the foundation of every modern tale of horror: L. Ron Hubbard's immortal *Fear*. It was rightly proclaimed by Stephen King as one of the very few works to genuinely warrant that overworked term "classic"—as in: *"This is a classic tale of creeping, surreal menace and horror. . . . This is one of the really, really good ones."*

L. Ron Hubbard, 1948, among fellow science fiction luminaries at the World Science Fiction Convention in Toronto.

To accommodate the greater body of L. Ron Hubbard fantasies, Street & Smith inaugurated *Unknown*—a classic pulp if there ever was one, and wherein readers were soon thrilling to the likes of *Typewriter in the Sky* and *Slaves of Sleep* of which Frederik Pohl would declare: *"There are bits and pieces from Ron's work that became part of the language in ways that very few other writers managed."*

And, indeed, at J. W. Campbell Jr.'s insistence, Ron was regularly drawing on themes from the Arabian Nights and so introducing readers to a world of genies, jinn, Aladdin and Sinbad—all of which, of course, continue to float through cultural mythology to this day.

At least as influential in terms of post-apocalypse stories was L. Ron Hubbard's 1940 *Final Blackout*. Generally acclaimed as the finest anti-war novel of the decade and among the ten best works of the genre ever authored—here, too, was a tale that would live on in ways few other writers imagined.

Portland, Oregon, 1943; L. Ron Hubbard, captain of the US Navy subchaser PC 815.

Hence, the later Robert Heinlein verdict: "Final Blackout *is as perfect a piece of science fiction as has ever been written.*"

Like many another who both lived and wrote American pulp adventure, the war proved a tragic end to Ron's sojourn in the pulps. He served with distinction in four theaters and was highly decorated for commanding corvettes in the North Pacific. He was also grievously wounded in combat, lost many a close friend and colleague and thus resolved to say farewell to pulp fiction and devote himself to what it had supported these many years—namely, his serious research.

But in no way was the LRH literary saga at an end, for as he wrote some thirty years later, in 1980:

"Recently there came a period when I had little to do. This was novel in a life so crammed with busy years, and I decided to amuse myself by writing a novel that was pure science fiction."

That work was *Battlefield Earth: A Saga of the Year 3000.* It was an immediate *New York Times* bestseller and, in fact, the first international science fiction blockbuster in decades. It was not, however, L. Ron Hubbard's magnum opus, as that distinction is generally reserved for his next and final work: The 1.2 million word *Mission Earth.*

> **Final Blackout**
> *is as perfect a piece of science fiction as has ever been written.*
>
> —Robert Heinlein

How he managed those 1.2 million words in just over twelve months is yet another piece of the L. Ron Hubbard legend. But the fact remains, he did indeed author a ten-volume *dekalogy* that lives in publishing history for the fact that each and every volume of the series was also a *New York Times* bestseller.

Moreover, as subsequent generations discovered L. Ron Hubbard through republished works and novelizations of his screenplays, the mere fact of his name on a cover signaled an international bestseller. . . . Until, to date, sales of his works exceed hundreds of millions, and he otherwise remains among the most enduring and widely read authors in literary history. Although as a final word on the tales of L. Ron Hubbard, perhaps it's enough to simply reiterate what editors told readers in the glory days of American Pulp Fiction:

He writes the way he does, brothers, because he's been there, seen it and done it!

THE STORIES FROM THE GOLDEN AGE

Your ticket to adventure starts here with the Stories from the Golden Age collection by master storyteller L. Ron Hubbard. These gripping tales are set in a kaleidoscope of exotic locales and brim with fascinating characters, including some of the most vile villains, dangerous dames and brazen heroes you'll ever get to meet.

The entire collection of over one hundred and fifty stories is being released in a series of eighty books and audiobooks. For an up-to-date listing of available titles, go to www.goldenagestories.com.

AIR ADVENTURE

Arctic Wings   *Man-Killers of the Air*
The Battling Pilot   *On Blazing Wings*
Boomerang Bomber   *Red Death Over China*
The Crate Killer   *Sabotage in the Sky*
The Dive Bomber   *Sky Birds Dare!*
Forbidden Gold   *The Sky-Crasher*
Hurtling Wings   *Trouble on His Wings*
The Lieutenant Takes the Sky   *Wings Over Ethiopia*

FAR-FLUNG ADVENTURE

SEA ADVENTURE

TALES FROM THE ORIENT

The Devil—With Wings   *Pearl Pirate*
The Falcon Killer   *The Red Dragon*
Five Mex for a Million   *Spy Killer*
Golden Hell   *Tah*
The Green God   *The Trail of the Red Diamonds*
Hurricane's Roar   *Wind-Gone-Mad*
Inky Odds   *Yellow Loot*
Orders Is Orders

MYSTERY

The Blow Torch Murder   *The Grease Spot*
Brass Keys to Murder   *Killer Ape*
Calling Squad Cars!   *Killer's Law*
The Carnival of Death   *The Mad Dog Murder*
The Chee-Chalker   *Mouthpiece*
Dead Men Kill   *Murder Afloat*
The Death Flyer   *The Slickers*
Flame City   *They Killed Him Dead*

127

FANTASY

SCIENCE FICTION

WESTERN

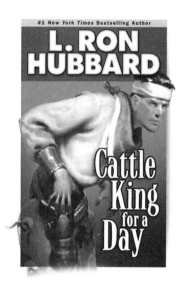

JOIN THE PULP REVIVAL
America in the 1930s and 40s

Pulp fiction was in its heyday and 30 million readers were regularly riveted by the larger-than-life tales of master storyteller L. Ron Hubbard. For this was pulp fiction's golden age, when the writing was raw and every page packed a walloping punch.

That magic can now be yours. An evocative world of nefarious villains, exotic intrigues, courageous heroes and heroines—a world that today's cinema has barely tapped for tales of adventure and swashbucklers.

Enroll today in the Stories from the Golden Age Club and begin receiving your monthly feature edition selected from more than 150 stories in the collection.

You may choose to enjoy them as either a paperback or audiobook for the special membership price of $9.95 each month along with FREE shipping and handling.

CALL TOLL-FREE: 1-877-8GALAXY
(1-877-842-5299) OR GO ONLINE TO
www.goldenagestories.com
AND BECOME PART OF THE PULP REVIVAL!

Prices are set in US dollars only. For non-US residents, please call
1-323-466-7815 for pricing information. Free shipping available for US residents only.

Galaxy Press, 7051 Hollywood Blvd., Suite 200, Hollywood, CA 90028